MW00976630

## No Way Out

Bunch was locked onto Lucky like a pair of vise grips. Lucky knew it was time to do some friendly talking. "Listen ... uh ... Bunch. Could you tell me your first name? I hate to call you—"

"Shut up."

Lucky was now moving, his feet touching the ground at times, but he was mostly just floating along under Bunch's power. Finally, in the middle of a snow-covered basketball court, Bunch came to a stop.

Most of the kids who were playing charged over to see what Bunch was up to. "He's going to tear that kid's head off," someone yelled. Other kids thought arms or legs or lungs were more likely.

"Listen, Bunch," Lucky pleaded, "I need to talk to you."

"No talk. Let's fight."

*Best wishes!*

*Dean Hughes*

## BOOKS BY DEAN HUGHES

### From Deseret Book

*The Lucky books*
Lucky's Crash Landing
Lucky Breaks Loose
Lucky's Gold Mine
Lucky Fights Back
Lucky's Mud Festival

*The Williams family historical novels*
Under the Same Stars
As Wide as the River
Facing the Enemy
Cornbread and Prayer

*Other titles*
Brothers
Hooper Haller
Jenny Haller
The Mormon Church, a Basic History

### From other publishers

*The Nutty books*
Nutty for President
Nutty and the Case of the Mastermind Thief
Nutty and the Case of the Ski-Slope Spy
Nutty Can't Miss
Nutty Knows All
Nutty, the Movie Star

*The Angel Park All-Stars* series
and
*The Angel Park Soccer Stars* series

*Other titles*
Jelly's Circus
Family Pose (*paperback titled* Family Picture)

# LUCKY
## FIGHTS BACK

# LUCKY
# FIGHTS BACK

## DEAN HUGHES

CINNAMON
TREE™

Published by
Deseret Book Company
Salt Lake City, Utah

*For Michael and Karen Hill,*
*and Candice, Capri,*
*Jacob, and Charity*

© 1991 Dean Hughes

All rights reserved. No part of this book may be reproduced
in any form or by any means without permission in writing
from the publisher, Deseret Book Company, P.O. Box 30178,
Salt Lake City, Utah 84130. This work is not an official
publication of The Church of Jesus Christ of Latter-day Saints.

Deseret Book is a registered trademark of Deseret Book Company.

**Library of Congress Cataloging-in-Publication Data**

Hughes, Dean, 1943–
    Lucky fights back / Dean Hughes.
        p.   cm.
    "Cinnamon tree."
    Summary: While staying in a Boston suburb with a family of
Mormons like himself, eleven-year-old Lucky tries to break through
the shell of their unfriendly son while enduring unwanted attention
from the local bully.
    ISBN 0-87579-559-5
    1. Friendship–Fiction.   2. Bullies–Fiction.   3. Conduct of
life–Fiction   4. Boston (Mass.)–Fiction.   5. Mormons–Fiction.]
I. Title.
PZ7.H87312Luf   1991
[Fic]–dc20                                                      91-31416
                                                                     CIP
                                                                      AC

Printed in the United States of America
10   9   8   7   6   5   4   3   2   1

# CHAPTER 1

*T*hough Lucky had spent an entire day at his new school, he still hadn't found anyone who seemed a likely candidate to be his friend. And then, as he walked out of the building, he ran right into an opportunity.

A kid the size of a full-grown buffalo was leaning over a small boy, and the big one was snorting smoke. Actually, it was steam, since the day was very cold, but it looked like smoke. "Bernie, I'm going to trample you," the big guy said. "I'm going to flatten your face."

Maybe that was a natural desire. The big guy had the flattest face Lucky had ever seen. His nose barely rose above the surface, like a buffalo chip on a desert plain. He was wearing a shaggy brown coat, and his ragged hair hung in his face and over his ears.

1

Kids were gathering from all directions to get in on the action. Lucky stepped close and tapped the buffalo on the shoulder. Somewhere in the crowd a boy said, "Don't be crazy. That's *Bunch!*"

Lucky looked up at the big fellow, who had turned around and was now leaning over him, blotting out the sky. Steam was still spouting from his nostrils. "Excuse me," Lucky said. "Would it really be fair for a guy your size to beat up on someone so small?"

"Okay. I'll fight both of you."

That wasn't at all what Lucky had in mind.

"Come and watch!" someone yelled. "Bunch is going to tromp on two guys at once." A cheer went up from the circle of kids.

Lucky was a little annoyed by their enthusiasm. "No, I don't want to fight," he said. "Let's just talk this over. Is Bunch your actual name?"

"What of it, metal mouth?"

Lucky did have braces, and he was an odd-looking boy. He was small for a sixth grader, and he seemed the sort of kid who would do better at a science fair than in a fist fight. His front teeth stuck out, and the wires flashed when he spoke. He didn't like being teased about that, but he decided, in this situation, to let the insult go by.

"Is that your first name or —"

Someone said, "It's his only name." Bunch himself had a different response, though. He grabbed Lucky's coat with one hand and Bernie's with the other, and he slammed the two boys together, shoulder to shoulder.

"Wait. Wait," Lucky shouted. "I wasn't smarting off. I only asked whether you really wanted to hurt this guy."

"Why wouldn't I?"

It was a good question. For all Lucky knew, this Bernie kid could be a thug or a terrorist. Maybe Bunch had caught him trying to blow up the school. Still, Lucky said, "Because you're bigger than he is."

"I'm bigger than everybody!"

Bunch had a point. If he could only beat up guys his size or bigger, he'd have to go looking for NFL linemen.

"But what did he do to you?" Lucky asked.

"He was following me."

For the first time, Bernie proved to have a voice—though it wasn't much more than a squeak right now. "I ride on the same bus, Bunch. I was just—"

"I told you yesterday not to follow me."

"I know. And I'm . . . really sorry. I won't . . . do it again."

Bunch had begun to bounce the two boys off the ground, pulling them up with a fist gripping each of their coats.

"Come on, Bunch," a boy behind Lucky yelled. "Bust 'em up." Lots of other kids yelled the same sort of encouragement. Bunch hesitated. Maybe he was worried about his honor. After all, either boy was only about the size of one of his legs.

Lucky thought it was about time to negotiate a settlement. "Bunch, we don't want to fight. Bernie already said he was sorry, and I certainly don't—"

Just then Bernie jumped back and tugged hard. He caught Bunch by surprise and managed to pull loose. Bunch responded by trying to grab him with both hands. Bernie stumbled back, got his balance, and was gone. He shot through the crowd like a running back.

Lucky, too, was already moving, and fortunately Bunch's reactions were slow. Lucky jumped into the crowd, used a couple of kids as unintentional blockers, and then he shot up the street in the same direction that Bernie had run.

Bernie was either very fast or very scared. He was leaving Lucky way behind. All the same, Lucky was chugging hard, and he felt sure that he had made his escape . . . until his legs tangled with each other. He hit the icy sidewalk on his chest and skidded along for several feet. His breath whooshed out. He was stunned, yet that was not his greatest fear: any second he expected to feel buffalo hooves trampling him. He rolled over and jumped up, ready for the one-man stampede. Bunch, however, was not behind him.

"It's okay," Bernie yelled from the corner. "He's not coming after us."

Lucky took a couple of deep breaths. His head was still spinning, but he turned and walked on to the corner, where Bernie was waiting.

"The bus is coming," Bernie said. "Bunch hates to miss the bus."

"Won't you miss it too?" Lucky asked.

"Yeah. But if I get on the bus, I'll miss my head. And I need my head more than a bus ride." Suddenly he grinned. Now that the color was returning to Bernie's face, Lucky could see that he had lots of freckles. His two front teeth angled away from each other, which gave him a snaky, mischievous look. His eyes were especially bright, as though the excitement had been great fun. "I *was* following him," he said.

"What?"

"I was walking really close behind him, just to

bug him. I did it yesterday and it made him mad, so I walked even closer today."

"Why?"

"I just like to bother him. He's ashamed to beat me up because I'm so little. I would have been all right if you hadn't come along. What the heck did you think you were doing anyway?"

"Trying to help you."

"Yeah, well, did you hear me crying? Next time, maybe you ought to think before you start interfering."

Lucky stared at Bernie. He had almost sacrificed his life for this kid, and now the guy was telling him . . .

"Who are you anyway?"

"Bernie, I don't think you should—"

"My name's Bernard. Only Bunch calls me Bernie."

"Bernard?"

"Not Bern-ARD. BERN-erd. The way the British say it."

"Okay, but I don't think—"

"So what's your name?"

"Lucky. Lucky Ladd."

"That's your name? It sounds like something you'd call a dog."

"My dad calls me Lucky, all right? It's sort of a

long story why." Normally, Lucky took this chance to tell about the car wreck his family had been in on the day he was born. Lucky's dad had considered the crash a good omen—since no one got hurt all that seriously—and he had tagged Lucky with the nickname. Yet Lucky was a little at a loss for words right now, and rather irritated.

"Did you just move in or something?" Bernard asked.

"Yeah, I did."

"Where from?"

"Well, from all over the place. We move every few weeks."

"Why?"

Patiently Lucky said, "My dad's an insurance man. Whenever there's a big problem—a disaster of some kind—he comes in and helps the local people take care of all the claims and stuff."

"Disaster? We haven't had any disasters, have we?"

"Yeah. That big fire in Boston."

"Oh, down there. How come you're living clear up here in Rockbridge?"

"We live in an RV—you know, a motor home. It's easier to park out here and take the train than it is to park downtown."

"You live in an RV?"

"Well, yeah. We travel so much that we—"

"Sure. I get the idea. But it's weird."

"Not really. It's just—"

"Hey, how many people do you know who camp out year round? I think that's pretty weird."

"Whatever." Lucky was starting to see why Bunch wanted to punch this kid.

"So where's your RV parked?"

"We're just parked in a driveway. My dad has some friends here. Their house is just a couple of blocks up—"

"Whose house?"

Lucky didn't know why Bernard needed to know so much—or why he couldn't let a person finish a sentence. "It's just a family," he said. "Their name is Christiansen. My dad has known them since—"

"Are you kidding? You're not talking about Michael Christiansen's house, are you?"

"Yeah. He's one of the—"

"He's just the richest kid around here, that's all. He went to our school last year. His dad drives the biggest Mercedes I've ever seen."

"Yeah, I know. He works for—"

"Are you going there now?"

"Yeah."

"Hey, I'll walk with you and call my mom from there. She'll be impressed."

Lucky nodded, though he had the feeling he was making a mistake.

"So how long are you going to be around?" Bernard asked. His tone was suddenly very different, as though he and Lucky were old friends.

"Two or three weeks."

"Well, look. Why don't we hang around together while you're here?"

Lucky shrugged. He was trying to think of an excuse. "I don't know if I—"

"If Bunch kills us both, we could maybe have our funerals together." Bernard laughed in a burst of little shrieks.

To Lucky's ears, the laugh was like fingernails on a chalkboard. For now, though, he was more interested in the funerals. "Look," Lucky said, "what do you think might happen tomorrow? Will Bunch still be after us?"

"He'll probably say some stuff—and threaten us. I think we're okay, though. He's probably embarrassed to wipe us out—even two of us together."

"I know. But we made him look pretty stupid. He might—"

"Oh, no. He didn't need any help. He can

handle 'stupid' by himself." Bernard was suddenly thrown into a fit of little screams again. Then he added, "Hey, if you want, I can teach you karate so you can defend yourself."

"Uh . . . no thanks," Lucky said. "I think I'll just try to make friends with the guy. That might be—"

"Friends? Are you kidding? Friends with Bunch? Oh, wow. Lucky, you must be as stupid as you look."

Lucky was usually a talkative kid, and friendly, but he found himself losing interest in this conversation—fast. Nonetheless, as the two boys walked up the hill, Bernard had lots of questions. And Lucky answered. The only trouble was, Bernard never had the patience to wait for the whole answer. Lucky had to fight back the urge not to tell Bernard to stop interrupting. Finally he decided to ask his own questions. "Do you live close to Bunch?"

"Oh no," Bernard said. "We live in the same direction, but the bus goes through a nice neighborhood—mine—and then to a bad one—Bunch's. Bunch comes from the worst family in our whole school. He and his brother are the meanest kids in . . . well, probably in the universe . . . but very definitely, in this town."

Lucky wondered what would make Bunch act that way. "Do you think Bunch sort of feels that—"

"My family is pretty rich," Bernard continued, without noticing that Lucky had said anything. "We've got a nice house and stuff like that. We're just not in the same league with the Christiansens, though. You don't have a phone in your RV, do you?"

"No."

"Good. I want to go inside the Christiansens' house and check it out."

Lucky nodded, though he was a little nervous about going inside. The Christiansens had been very nice to Lucky and his dad. They had invited them to dinner the first night. Yet Lucky liked the RV better. Part of the problem was that Michael, who was a seventh grader, didn't seem very friendly. Besides, everything was so perfect in the house that Lucky worried about messing something up.

"My mom says that the Christiansens are Mormons. Did you know that?"

"Yeah. I'm a Mormon too."

"No kidding? The only Mormons I ever heard of are quarterbacks. Do you know Ty Detmer and Jim McMahon and all those guys?"

"Not personally. Jim McMahon's not a Mormon, though. He just played for—"

"Sure he is. He played for BYU. That's a Mormon school."

"I know. But not everybody—"

"Oh, wow, look at that house."

They had arrived. Lucky was gritting his teeth to keep from saying what he was thinking. He took Bernard to the front door and rang the doorbell. Bernard wanted to know why they couldn't just walk in, but Lucky didn't feel that he could do that.

Sister Christiansen let Bernard use the telephone, and she was very nice to him, even though he never stopped talking. When he finished his call, he told her, "Mom knows where you live. Everybody does. This is some house. I'll bet it cost some big bucks."

"Thank you. We—"

"Ours is nice but not like this. I'll bet you could play a game of touch football in this living room."

Lucky thought maybe Sister Christiansen was gritting her teeth too, though she didn't show it. She said, "Well, stop by and see us again some time."

"Don't worry. I will," Bernard said, walking out the door. "I know Michael. He's sort of a friend of mine."

Then, as soon as the door was shut, he turned

to Lucky and said, "Let me have a look at your RV before my mom comes."

Lucky led Bernard to the RV. In back of the house, the driveway opened into a wide area in front of a three-car garage. Lucky's dad had parked the RV along the edge of the pavement, near some tall maple trees that were now without leaves.

"Hey, this place is cool," Bernard told Lucky as he stepped inside. "Maybe I'll sleep over with you one night. That'd be a lot of fun."

"Well, we don't have a lot of—"

"I'm glad we're going to be friends. My mom would like it if I started hanging around with Michael Christiansen. So would Dad. He always likes to make good business contacts."

That's how the conversation continued—with Bernard in control. Lucky wondered how this whole thing had happened. Lucky always picked a friend in each of the places he lived. This time, though, someone had picked him, and he wasn't sure he was happy about that. Maybe Bunch would have been a better choice.

One good thing, though. Lucky had a habit of talking too much, and Dad always told him to be careful about taking over conversations. At least that wouldn't be a problem with Bernard around. So maybe that was lucky. Lucky's dad always said that people could find some good luck in every situation if they just looked for it. And Lucky usually found that to be true.

When Bernard's mom drove into the driveway, Bernard climbed down the RV steps, then turned around. "Hey, see you in the morning, Lucky. We had a good time. Maybe tomorrow we can bug old Bunch some more."

Lucky had no response for that. He just shook his head. Maybe this was one situation where even Dad couldn't find a whole lot of good luck.

# CHAPTER 2

Lucky talked things over with his dad that night. They were eating in the RV, even though the Christiansens had asked them in for dinner. Dad told Sister Christiansen that he and Lucky needed to keep their family life as normal as possible, but Lucky knew his dad was embarrassed to "sponge" off his old friend—even if the man could afford to feed the whole town.

So Lucky and his father ate tuna sandwiches and carrot sticks in the motor home, and Lucky was glad of it. While they ate, Lucky told his dad about his little adventure that day.

"So you just went up and told this kid to lay off?" Dad asked. He laughed in a low sort of rumble—not one of his usual bone-buster kind of laughs.

"Well, no. I saw he was picking on this little

15

guy, and I didn't think that was fair. So I just asked
him to lay off."

"And how big was this little guy? About your
size?"

Lucky thought about that. "Well, yeah. He may
be an inch or two taller than me, but—"

This time Dad cracked off a good laugh that
rattled the bottles in Lucky's bug collection.

"Hey, I told you, I just asked him. I didn't
threaten to punch him or anything like that."

"What grade is this Bunch guy in?"

"Sixth."

"What about Bernard."

"It's BERN-erd."

"So what grade is BERN-erd in?"

"Sixth. But Bunch is about the same size as . . . I
don't know . . . maybe a big forward in the NBA."

"I get the picture. Mailman Malone," his dad
said and nodded, though he was still grinning. "You
could get yourself murdered, Son. I'm a big guy,
but I wouldn't mess with the Mailman, and you sure
shouldn't mess with this Bunch kid."

"I know that, Dad. So what do I do now?"

"Just tell him you don't want any trouble. And
if he still keeps bothering you, tell the principal."

"Is that what you would have done when you
were a kid?"

Lucky's father laughed again, though it was more of a chuckle. "Well, no. I was stupid. I probably would have punched the big guy and ended up with my nose on the wrong side of one of my eyes. Now don't you do that."

"Why not? Don't you think I can take care of myself?"

"Lucky, I hate to say it, but you'd probably miss him and hit yourself in the nose." Dad took a fake swing and pretended to bonk himself. He was a big man, and when he flattened out his nose that way, the resemblance to Bunch was not something Lucky liked to think about.

Lucky did know that his dad had a point, however. His own clumsiness was what usually got him into messes. This time, though, the danger was "out there," and Lucky wasn't sure he could talk his way out of it.

"Lucky, don't fight him, no matter what," Dad said. "Talk to him. If you appeal to the best in people, they usually respond."

"This guy isn't your usual sort of kid. I think he mashes people first and talks later."

"Well, I'll tell you what. I don't believe that. He's big, and maybe he's no genius. I'll also bet he's not such a bad guy, once you give him a chance. That's what you'll find with just about everybody."

Lucky really wanted to believe that—it just seemed the right way to think about things. His father hadn't seen Bunch, however, or heard him. "I don't know, Dad. I hope you're right."

"Sure I am. Just get acquainted with him. Talk to him. Be his friend. He probably acts that way because no one is nice to him."

"Okay," Lucky said, and he nodded. "I'll try that." He really did like to think his dad was right.

"One thing," Lucky's father added, "if talking doesn't work, I think I'd try ducking and running again." He launched off another one of his bomb-drop laughs. "You know, show him a lot of love and friendship—but kind of stay out of his reach."

Lucky grinned. Dad could almost always make him feel better, no matter what happened. Still, he had his doubts about their stay in Rockbridge. "Are we going to be around here long?" he asked.

"No. Three weeks, tops, I'd say."

"Wasn't the fire very bad?"

"Yeah, it was bad. Very bad." His father suddenly looked serious. "A whole lot of people are out of their homes. And they're poor people—people who didn't have much to start with."

"Where are they staying?"

"Well, that's just the problem. It's cold out, and homeless shelters are full. Most of them are crowded into an old gymnasium. I've been trying to find a better place. I'd like to see them into permanent housing before Christmas. That gives us only about a month, so it won't be easy."

"Is that your job—to find places for them?"

"Sort of, I guess."

Lucky knew it wasn't. Dad had already told him that most of the people didn't have insurance. But then, that was nothing new for him. He always did more for people than his job really required.

The next morning Lucky was happy to find that things seemed okay. He didn't see Bunch outside, and Bunch and Lucky were in different classes. Even better, Bernard wasn't in Lucky's class either.

Lucky liked his teacher. She was the happy, wild sort who always sounded excited, even if the class was about to work on "algebra readiness." Her name was Ms. Parlucci, and she could have been twenty or fifty—Lucky wasn't sure which.

Lucky had a way of getting into a new school just in time for a unit on the Civil War. He didn't mind; he found the war interesting. Today, though, when Ms. Parlucci mentioned the number of casualties, a kid with a flat-top haircut leaned over from his desk and said, "That's what you're going to be before this day is over. A casualty. A Bunch casualty." Then he laughed.

Lucky's sense of security suddenly vanished. He tried not to look scared, but the rest of the day he found himself waiting for the ax to drop. Still, he told himself that his dad was right. He just had to talk things out with Bunch and be friendly. Why would the guy want to hurt him?

Lucky didn't see Bunch at recess, or in the cafeteria. He did see Bernard, who explained that Bunch had second lunch.

"I wouldn't worry," Bernard told Lucky. "If you don't want to mess with him, let's just go out the back door after school and sneak around the building. Then we can walk to your place."

Lucky was trying to eat a mouthful of something green that might have been meat or maybe Jell-O. It was turning into rubber in his mouth. Actually, Bunch was only part of the problem.

"Bernard, Dad told me not to go into the Christiansens' house too much." That wasn't true—not really—but it was the sort of thing Dad probably would say if the subject came up.

"Don't worry. I already told Mom to pick me up. I told her we were going to hang around for a while, but she didn't think that was a good idea because she doesn't know you guys, and you live in an RV and move around and everything. Then I said I would be with Michael Christiansen too, and so she said that would be okay."

"Bernard, Michael hasn't said more than four words to me since I got here. We're not going to be hanging around with—"

"Hey, I know. Michael wouldn't have a thing to do with a kid like you if you weren't living in his driveway. For one thing, you really don't dress well enough. But see, Mom doesn't know that."

Lucky glanced down at the T-shirt he was wearing. What was wrong with the way he dressed, for crying out loud? "Look, it's not like we're some kind of—"

"It would be good if we maybe tried to talk to Michael. Because I don't like to lie, if you know what I mean."

Lucky dropped the whole thing. He gazed around the lunch room and wondered whether there weren't some other guys he could get to know.

"Anyway, we can hang out in your RV for a while. That'll be cool."

Lucky nodded. "Yeah, right."

When school got out that afternoon, Lucky and Bernard headed for the back door. Lucky figured that talking to Bunch would be a good idea, the way his dad had suggested. Letting him cool off a couple more days over the weekend, though, couldn't hurt. And going out the back door definitely fit into the "out of reach" part of the plan.

In fact, the back-door approach might have been a great one, except for one thing. Bunch was waiting for them there. "I knew you'd try to sneak out the back door," he said in a huge voice. "How stupid do you think I am?"

Lucky froze, but Bernard said, "How stupid do I think you are? Well, let me think. I guess very doesn't quite cover it. And extremely isn't really strong enough. How about mega-stupid? That might be about right."

Lucky couldn't believe it. He didn't need this.

Bernard was already dancing to one side, and when Bunch grabbed for him, Bernard dodged and then ran for his life. Yet when Lucky tried to do the same, he slipped as he took off, and a big hand reached out and grabbed his coat by the shoulder. Lucky was jerked right off the ground.

Bunch yelled to the sprinting Bernard, "Come back, Bernie, or I'll kill your buddy."

Bernard, however, kept right on cruising until he got to the corner of the school. Then he turned around and yelled, "Lucky, make a break for it."

Bunch was locked onto Lucky like a pair of vise grips. Lucky knew it was time to do some real talking. Friendly talking. "Listen . . . uh . . . Bunch.

Could you tell me your first name? I hate to call you—"

"Shut up."

Lucky was now moving, his feet touching the ground at times, but he was mostly just floating along under Bunch's power. Lucky had no idea where they were going. In time, Bunch offered an explanation. "We gotta get farther away from the school before we fight."

Lucky supposed that meant that Bunch feared getting in trouble. It was good to know that he had respect for some sort of rules. Maybe he also didn't believe in eye-gouging.

Finally, somewhere in the middle of a snow-covered basketball court, Bunch came to a stop. Not far away was a short, steep hill, and then another flat area—probably a baseball field. From that upper playground area, kids had flattened the snow, and they had been running and sliding down the hill on their stomachs. Now most of the kids who were playing came charging over to see what Bunch was up to.

"He's going to tear that kid's head off," someone yelled. However, other kids thought arms or legs or lungs were more likely. Everyone seemed excited no matter what part of Lucky's body went first.

"Listen, Bunch, listen," Lucky pleaded, "I need to talk to you."

"No talk. Let's fight." Bunch grabbed Lucky by his other shoulder and jerked him around so that the two boys were facing each other. "Go ahead and swing at me."

Lucky couldn't have swung if he had wanted to. Bunch's grasp had turned his coat into a mummy bag. But he didn't think that was the most important point to make at the moment. "Bunch, I don't want to fight you," he said, and he tried to sound friendly and casual.

"Who does?" Bunch asked.

Lucky had no answer for that one. He tried again. "This is all a big misunderstanding. It was my opinion—but only my opinion—that maybe you shouldn't hurt Bernard. We all have a right to our own opinions, don't we? And actually I now know that Bernard can be very annoying, and maybe you lost your temper a little at the moment. I'm sure though you wouldn't hurt a kid about half—maybe a fourth—your size. And I also know you're a reasonable person who can—"

"Are you going to take the first swing or do I have to punch you in the stomach?"

The stomach? What a thought. Lucky suddenly felt sick.

"No, Bunch . . . or Mr. Bunch. Really. I don't want to fight. I don't like to fight. I'm not—"

"You're chicken to fight me; that's what you are."

This accusation brought cheers from the crowd. Lucky wanted to ask any of the kids if they'd like to give it a try. Once again, though, he decided now was not a good time to get off the subject. Lucky had to try another approach. He remembered what Bernard had said. "Listen, if you hurt me, everyone is going to call you a big bully."

"No, they won't. They don't dare."

The silence in the audience seemed to verify the truth of that one. Lucky had to hand it to Bunch; he knew what he knew. He tried a different tack. "Yesterday you were ready to fight two of us. Won't you look silly just fighting one? Maybe you should—"

"I'll take care of Bernie later."

Bunch let go of Lucky's right shoulder and said, "Okay, go ahead. Hit me right in the face as hard as you can."

It was an option. Lucky considered it for a whole microsecond. But he knew he had to appeal to Bunch's better nature. "Bunch, I'll bet we could be really good friends. In fact, if we hadn't met under such odd circumstances, I have the feeling we would probably really like each other. Why don't we start all over and just—"

At that moment fate stepped in and changed Lucky's entire future. Or maybe gave him one.

Just as Bunch doubled up his fist—*splat!*—a big wet snowball hit him right in the side of the head. For a second or two, time seemed to stop. The kids in the crowd took a collective breath—and waited.

Then a number of things happened very fast. Bunch seemed to realize the magnitude of the moment. Someone had actually hit him with a snowball. He released Lucky and stepped back to look for the madman who would think to do such a thing. At that exact moment, though, a little kid, maybe eight years old, was hurtling down the hill, sliding on his stomach. The innocent child could not have known that he was sliding into history. Yet there he was, a missile on a collision course with destiny—and Bunch.

Just as Bunch stepped back, the little kid slid into Bunch's leg. He must have hit him before he had planted his foot firmly because Bunch flipped in the air and came down sliding, carried by the momentum of the boy who was now under him. He and the kid slipped across the ice together for maybe ten feet, and then, *thonk!* Bunch's head hammered into the base of the basketball standard. It was an iron pole, and Bunch hit it square.

The boy was all right — and so was the pole — but Bunch was stunned. His eyes rolled back in his head, and for at least half a minute he seemed to lose touch with the world.

Kids had scattered, as though fleeing from a live grenade. They spun around, though, when they heard the thunk. And then they stood in stunned silence, waiting to see whether Bunch would ever get up — and who would have to pay, if he did. They were all on their toes, ready to run.

The little boy who had slid into Bunch rolled out from under him and sprinted out of the territory as fast as he could go. A kid on top of the hill also darted away like a scared rabbit. He must have been the one who had thrown the snowball. Lucky was sure he had never intended to hit Bunch. No one would do that on purpose.

When Bunch finally got his vision back, he was looking straight at Lucky, who was saying, "Are you all right?"

Bunch mumbled, "What did you do to me?"

"I didn't do anything. It was an accident."

Lucky suddenly realized that he was in bigger trouble than ever, though he had no idea how big until he heard someone yell, "That new kid beat up on Bunch."

"No, Bunch. No. That isn't true," Lucky insisted.

Lots of kids in the area could have backed Lucky up on that, yet no one did. Instead, they all waited and watched—probably hoping for some more action.

"See, a kid threw a snowball," Lucky said, "and then you stepped back to . . . " Lucky had a clear impression that Bunch wasn't listening. Bunch rolled over onto all fours, and then, slowly, he struggled upward. He was rising onto his hind legs when someone yelled, "Run, kid, run!"

And Lucky did. He lost his nerve—and his faith in reason. He knew he should try to talk to Bunch, but he also remembered Dad's "duck and run" advice, and now seemed the time for it. He ran all the way home.

When he got there, Bernard was nowhere to be found. Finally something had gone right.

# CHAPTER 3

**L**ucky had one thing to be thankful for: the weekend. Two extra days to live. And who knew? Maybe Bunch had a short attention span. Maybe he would forget the whole thing by Monday.

Then again, maybe not. Still, Lucky had two whole days to believe that everything would come out all right in the end.

When Dad asked what had happened, Lucky didn't really tell the whole story. Dad was the sort of guy who'd want to drive over to the Bunch house and talk things out. Somehow that didn't seem like the best answer right now.

Dad did have some advice: "Son, you've got to talk with this kid. That's always better than fighting."

Lucky really wanted to believe that. All the other choices weren't very appealing. And really, it

was the only thing that made sense. Somehow, he
had to have a good talk with Bunch. But that could
wait until later—say, Monday, or even a day or two
after that. Even a week might not be a bad idea.
Or maybe a letter after Lucky moved away. Yeah,
a letter. That might be the best plan of all. If Lucky
could just stay alive long enough to get far enough
away to write it.

Saturday morning Dad announced that the
Christiansens had offered to take them on a sight-
seeing tour around the Boston area. Normally,
Lucky would have been excited. However, as Michael came out of the house, Lucky heard him complaining. When Michael plunked himself in the car,
he was clearly in a black mood.

Brother Christiansen and Dad sat up front in
the big Mercedes, and Lucky ended up in the back,
in the middle, between Michael and his mother.
Sister Christiansen, though, was nice. She was classy
yet down to earth. And something in her voice
sounded like home—maybe even the mom that
Lucky remembered.

Brother Christiansen didn't act like a big shot
either. He had a fancy home and nice cars, but his
favorite thing to talk about was the good times he
and Dad had shared in Utah, growing up. They had
played basketball together in high school, and both

joked about all the one-sided games they had lost. Brother Christiansen was as tall as Dad, maybe a little taller, but he was slender. Dad made two of him.

Brother Christiansen drove into downtown Boston. Lucky kept looking out one window and then the other. Though he had been in a lot of places, more often than not his dad was busy, and they didn't really have time to see the local sights.

They parked in a garage near the big park called the "Boston Commons." Then they all followed a painted red line on the sidewalk that took them along the "Freedom Trail." Lucky liked seeing Paul Revere's grave and, later, his house. He especially liked visiting the Old North Church, where the lanterns had signalled that the British troops were coming.

Brother Christiansen knew a lot about Paul Revere. "Some other riders were just as important as Revere was," he told Lucky. "But all the others have been forgotten. As much as anything, Longfellow's poem was what made Revere famous. I guess it pays to advertise."

All this time, Michael tagged along, sitting down whenever he had a chance and complaining that he was tired or cold. It really was a cold day. With all the walking, though, Lucky hadn't been uncomfortable. Michael was tall, with long legs, and Lucky was the one who had to work to keep up with everyone.

Michael had on a designer ski jacket—with about six different colors—and ski gloves. He was also wearing a pair of athletic shoes that must have set someone back a couple of hundred bucks. He looked like his mother, with reddish hair and eyelashes so light that they almost disappeared, but he was built like his dad.

When the group left the Old North Church, Brother Christiansen told everyone that he knew a great little Italian restaurant nearby. He was taking them all to lunch. He strode out, in his usual way, with Dad right with him. When Michael lagged behind, Lucky decided to break the ice between them. He slowed up and walked with Michael.

"I guess you've seen this stuff a lot of times," Lucky said.

"Every time someone comes to visit, Dad drags us over here."

Lucky knew that Michael's two younger brothers and his older sister had been let off the hook this time. He was also sure that Michael had been forced to come along because he was closest to Lucky's age. "I'm sorry you had to come," he said.

Michael and Lucky were walking down a narrow

street in the Boston "North End," the Italian district. It was really colorful to Lucky, so old compared to anything in the West. Then Michael said, "My parents seem to have a thousand relatives each, and that many friends besides. Anyone who ever makes it to the east coast has to drop by to see us. And my dad thinks he has to walk the stupid Freedom Trail with every one of them." This was apparently offered to justify Michael's misery. It didn't exactly make for better feelings, though.

"I thought for once—in winter—we might get to skip the whole thing." He had hunched his shoulders and pulled his chin down into the neck of his parka as though he were freezing.

"Do you ever go out to Utah to visit?" Lucky said, trying to think of something else to say.

"Oh, yeah. Every year. Then we sit endlessly and listen to Dad and Mom talk to every relative who ever lived. The only good thing in Utah is the skiing. So when do we go? Usually in the summer when it's a hundred degrees every day. Utah has to be the most boring place on the planet."

Lucky liked getting home to Utah. Of course, he had lived there most of his life, and he had some cousins he had a lot of fun with. He didn't say that though. He tried something else. "So are you a Boston Celtics fan?"

Michael shrugged. "Not really."

"Where do they play?"

"Boston Garden. Down there." Michael nodded his head enough to indicate a general direction.

"Do you ever go to the games?"

"Once in a while."

"Larry Bird is really awesome. I'd like to—"

"I don't like basketball that much," Michael announced. But he seemed to be saying, "I don't want to talk about this—or anything else."

Lucky let it go. Yet he was bothered. He knew that some kids didn't take to him at first, but he could usually get them talking and find some common ground. It was something he always trusted in himself: that he could make friends with anyone. Maybe Michael didn't look or act much like Bunch—yet the results Lucky was getting were about the same. Still, Lucky decided to give the conversation a little rest and then try again.

The boys walked past a bakery, and Lucky looked in to see the Italian pastries. The sidewalk was not even, though, and Lucky caught his foot and tripped. He felt himself going over and tried to pull his hands from his coat pockets. But it was too late. He landed flat on his chest. For a moment, Lucky struggled to get his breath.

Michael knelt down by him. "Are you all right?" he said.

Lucky was hurt, but he was more embarrassed. He got up before he really wanted to. Michael even gave him a little help. For just a moment, the two looked at each other. Lucky saw some concern or . . . something besides the usual distance.

"I'm always doing stuff like that," Lucky said. "Dad says I have three left feet." He laughed, though he was still trying to get his breath.

Michael didn't laugh, and he seemed uncomfortable about the eye contact. He turned and walked away. Lucky hurried to keep up, which wasn't easy since he was still short of breath and his chest hurt.

They walked for maybe half a block without speaking. Then Michael asked, "What's going on between you and Bunch?" His tone made it sound as though Lucky and Bunch were old friends. Lucky was surprised Michael knew anything about that.

"Nothing much," Lucky said. "He just wants to kill me."

"If you think you can fight the guy, you're crazy."

That much Lucky could figure out by himself. "Hey, I don't want to fight him."

"The Bunches are nothing but scum."

Lucky caught something he hardly knew how to

respond to. Michael seemed to be implying that Lucky's "connection" to Bunch brought disgrace to Michael.

"Look, Michael, it's not like I've been sharing my lunch with the guy. I stuck up for a kid, and now Bunch is trying—"

"Well, just don't let him follow you home."

What was that supposed to mean? If Lucky got smashed all over the driveway, the blood stains might look bad on the concrete? Or a fight with "scum" at Michael's house would be bad for his image?

Maybe Lucky couldn't make friends with Michael. Maybe he didn't want to. Maybe this town was one to write off, and then he could just try harder in the next one. But that didn't work. No matter how much Michael bugged Lucky, he wanted to see if he couldn't break through his hard shell. The truth was, strange as it seemed, Lucky felt sorry for Michael. The kid just seemed so unhappy.

On Sunday morning Lucky and his dad went to church with the Christiansens. Brother Christiansen was a member of the high council, and he had an assignment away from the ward. So he drove everyone to church first—this time in their big van—and told Michael to take Lucky into the deacons quorum, then drove off. Lucky hadn't turned twelve yet, but Dad and Brother Christiansen had decided Lucky would be more comfortable with Michael than he would be in Primary.

Lucky expected the worst and hoped for the best. Unfortunately, he got what he expected. Michael treated Lucky like a tag-along who'd been forced upon him. He hardly said a word. In Sunday School the teacher asked Michael to introduce his friend.

Michael mumbled, "This is Lucky."

The teacher, Brother Sessions, was a young man, maybe twenty-five or so, and he was trying to be nice. He was one of those "Oh, won't Sunday School be fun today?" sort of people. Lucky thought he came on a little too strong when he said, "Your name is Lucky? Wow, what a great name. Are you?"

Lucky nodded and tried not to smile. He was always self-conscious when he met a new group of kids. His braces were supposed to fix up his buck teeth, sooner or later. For now, though, they only advertised the obvious.

"Where do you live?" Brother Sessions asked.

"Uh, well, actually . . . my dad moves every few weeks."

"Is the law after you or something?" Brother Sessions snorted as though he had gotten off a really good one.

Lucky stared at Brother Sessions's tie, which looked like a salad, and he avoided looking at anyone else. He explained about his dad's work and mentioned the fire in Boston. Lucky had always enjoyed telling about his life on the road. Most kids thought it sounded exciting. Now he knew Michael's attitude, and he suspected others in this group might feel the same.

"Well, Lucky, we're just more than happy to have you with us. We hope you'll feel very welcome while you're here. Are you staying with the Christiansens?"

"Sort of. We travel in a motor home. We're parked by their house."

Brother Sessions nodded. Someone sitting behind Lucky said, "Yeah, that's our local KOA campground," and everyone laughed.

Except Michael.

After that, Lucky got through the class without any more attention brought to him. But Priesthood started exactly the same way as Sunday School. The deacons quorum advisor asked the same kind of questions.

When Lucky got to sacrament meeting, he thought he had made it through. Afterwards though, as Lucky and his dad left the chapel, Sister Christiansen introduced Dad to some friends. Then they all stood in the foyer and talked. That's when one of Michael's friends walked over. Michael called him Dustin. He hadn't been in the deacons quorum; Lucky figured he must be older, maybe a teacher.

Dustin spoke to Michael, but he was looking at Lucky. "Hey, is this the kid my little brother told me about? The one who knocked Bunch down?"

Michael shrugged. Lucky said, "I didn't knock him down. Someone else did. It was an accident."

"I heard that he was going to punch you out, so you let him have it first, and he fell backwards and hit his head on the sidewalk."

"No, no. He hit his head on a basketball pole. I—"

"Man, you're nuts. He's going to shred your body into little pieces."

Lucky knew that may well be true. "Look, I didn't hit the guy. He's ten times my size. Somebody hit him with a snowball, and he stepped around, and—"

"All I know is, everyone says you punched him, and he told kids that he's going to make hamburger out of you."

Nice image.

"Look," Lucky said, "I'm just going to explain to him—"

"You don't explain anything to a guy like Bunch. If I were you, I'd get out of the area—fast." He laughed one of those break-in-the-middle laughs only a boy whose voice is changing can produce.

"I'll be okay," Lucky said, and he looked away. He wanted the subject to change.

"That's what you think. I'm serious. If I were you, I'd drop out of school and head back home— wherever that is." He was laughing. At the same time, he had a cocky way of holding his head back and rolling it from side to side, as if he were some great authority on the subject.

Then Michael said, "Hey, they live in an RV. They don't have a home to go back to." Michael had a way of making things that Lucky had always rather liked suddenly seem embarrassing.

"You don't have a house anywhere?" Dustin asked.

"No. Not anymore. We stay on the road all the time. It's part of my dad's business."

"So what do you do, pull into trailer parks or something?"

"Sometimes. Or next to insurance offices—"

"Or in my driveway," Michael said. He and Dustin both laughed.

That's when Dustin said, "Well, you finally made it into a nice neighborhood."

Lucky said rather lamely, "Traveling around is kind of interesting."

"Yeah, and look at it this way," Michael said. "He's trained to be a truck driver when he grows up."

"Yeah. Or he could work for a circus."

Dustin and Michael thought that was very funny.

Lucky didn't. But he tried to smile. He didn't want these guys to know they were getting to him.

# CHAPTER 4

After church Lucky and his dad had dinner with the Christiansens even though Lucky hinted that he'd rather eat Dad's usual Sunday Shake 'n' Bake chicken dinner. Actually, though, Lucky had a nice time. Emily, Michael's older sister, was very interested to hear about life on the road, and she seemed enchanted with all the experiences they could tell about. It didn't hurt any, either, that she was fifteen and a real knockout. She had long, blonde hair and a smile that kept making Lucky forget his stories.

The two little brothers, Greg and Jed, were outright jealous of Lucky's vagabond life, and the parents kept saying that they'd like to try it for a year—just to escape the constant pressure they were under. Only Michael remained uninterested. He said nothing, and he got up and left the room as soon as dinner was over. Lucky didn't see him again.

Later, when Dad and Lucky went back to the RV, Lucky lay on his bed—which was also the only couch in their "house." He did some reading, but he couldn't seem to get his mind to stop returning to what had happened at church. Michael seemed to be going out of his way to be unfriendly, and Lucky just couldn't figure out why. The only thing he was sure of was that the guy was miserable himself, and he seemed to want to make everyone else feel the same way.

"What's the trouble, Son?" Dad asked.

Lucky didn't want to talk about it. For one thing, he didn't want his dad to feel awkward with Brother Christiansen. "Nothing," Lucky said. "I'm just tired."

"You and Michael aren't hitting it off too well, are you?"

"No. But that doesn't matter."

Dad sat down at the kitchen table—which was also part of the "living room." Lucky had never really thought how cramped the RV was. The Christiansens had two family rooms, either one of which was three times bigger than the entire motor home.

"How was church?" Dad asked.

"Just about like always."

"Well, I'll tell you something, Lucky," Dad said. "If you ever have to make a living as an undercover agent, you're in big trouble. You're the worst liar I've ever heard. When that old motor mouth of yours shuts down, I know, just like that, that something's wrong."

"I'm not lying. Church was just like always."

"Do you like being here?"

"Not much. We won't be around long, though."

"What gives? You usually like the places we go to. You almost always want to stay longer."

"I know."

"Come on, Lucky. Tell me what's going on."

Lucky took a deep breath. He wasn't sure what to tell his dad. A lot was going on—including life with Bunch, which would start again in the morning. So Lucky avoided all that by asking, "How did Brother Christiansen get so rich?"

"Why?"

"I was just wondering."

"Well, he graduated from BYU. Then he came out here to the Harvard business school. He got a masters degree, and then got a job with East/West Systems, a big corporation. You know, a management job. He and Julie moved to Texas for a while, and then to Georgia. He finally ended up back up here in the head office. And now he's president of the company."

"Why didn't you do something like that?"

Dad laughed—softly for once. "Is that what this is about?"

"No. I was just wondering."

"Well, it's funny. I sometimes ask myself the same thing. In high school I always got better grades than John did. Even in college we did about the same. When I graduated, I thought about maybe getting an MBA, going to a big-name school the way he did, but—well, I don't know—I really wanted to be a teacher. That's what I did at first. I waited quite a while before I got married, and then, once you were coming along, I was starting to see that I would never make a very good living as a teacher. By then I'd started selling insurance on the side—and gradually I moved in that direction."

"How come I never had any brothers or sisters?"

"Your mom fought the cancer for a long time, Lucky. You weren't even a year old when we first found out she had it."

Lucky saw Dad look down at the table, his eyes half closed. Lucky knew that look so well.

"Couldn't we make more money if you stayed home and sold insurance?" Lucky asked.

"Sure, we could."

"Could we be sort of rich by now?"

Dad smiled. "Well, if I had stayed on a steady pace, we would have been pretty well off. Those last couple of years, though, when I knew the cancer would take your mom sooner or later, I didn't push as hard. I wanted to be with her—and then at the end—I had to be with her. You and I would've been a lot better off if we had stayed put. I just didn't have the heart to stay in our house. When I got this chance to travel, it seemed like a good idea."

"Are we going to go back to Utah someday?"

"I don't know, Son. Would you like to?"

"Maybe."

"I'll tell you one thing, Lucky. I'm actually making good money. It doesn't seem like it, since we're in this RV all the time. I get a lot of travel money, and we don't spend much of it. I've been putting money away. When it comes time for you to go to college, you can do what you want. If you want to do what John did, I could help you."

"I couldn't make it to Harvard. I'm average. That's what you always tell me."

Dad cracked off a pretty good laugh—about a four on the Richter scale, but no damage was done. "Hey, you're an average very smart kid. You've got the ability to do anything you want to do."

Lucky was surprised. He never thought of himself as being all that smart. "How can you be average and very smart?"

Dad laughed again, louder. "Well, when I tell you that you're average, I mean that you're a regular kid. That doesn't mean you can't accomplish a lot in your life. Look at John. He's a wealthy man now, yet he and Julie are just regular folks—the same as they always were."

"Michael's not."

Dad's eyes suddenly focused in on Lucky. "Ahh. So that's what this is all about. Has Michael been looking down his nose at you?"

Lucky thought about denying it. Then he said, "Uh . . . sort of, I guess."

"What did he say?"

"He and that other kid, Dustin, were making fun of us for living in an RV."

Dad nodded. After a time he said, "The children of people who do well are the ones who sometimes lose track of where they came from. That's not entirely their fault. It's hard for them to get the right perspective on this world."

Lucky thought that was probably right.

"Michael ought to meet the people I've been working with this week. These are families who had almost nothing, and they lost what they had. Most of them are hard workers, but they don't have much education or training. They get laid off when times are hard. Then every time they start to get a leg up, something seems to go wrong again."

Dad wasn't much of one to talk with his hands. He had learned that the big things got in his way enough without waving his arms around. But now he patted his palms on the table. "We have a nice home here, Lucky—strange as it is—and we have a very interesting life. What's wrong is not that we have so little; it's that maybe some kids have too much, and then they can't handle it."

"So I guess we're lucky, huh?" Lucky said, and he smiled. "Poor people are unlucky, and rich people are unlucky. It's guys like us who have it made."

This time Dad gave the RV a good jolt. His laugh made the whole place pitch and roll. "That's exactly right," Dad said with a huge grin.

And Lucky did feel better. He told himself he would forget about Michael and Dustin and not let them get to him again. Of course, that didn't solve the other problem. The next morning Lucky had to face the faceless giant, Bunch. And Bunch, by now, probably wanted to make Lucky's face look like his own.

Dad was still on the old subject. "Hey," he said,

"look at it this way," and he laughed at his own joke before he made it. "You're improving Michael's image."

"What?"

"Everyone who drives by here probably says, 'Look at that. The Christiansens have everything else. Now they've gone out and bought a nice big motor home.'"

"Not if they see us getting in and out of it," Lucky said.

"That won't matter. People will probably think we're the hired help."

It wasn't really that funny, though it cracked Dad up, but Lucky found himself laughing too. Lucky could never hold back when his dad started laughing.

That night Lucky wrote postcards to lots of his friends. Among others, he wrote to Jared, Cal, and Tiffany in California; Malcolm and Sharon in Louisiana; and Bobby in West Yellowstone. He was getting too many kids on his list, and keeping up with everyone was hard.

Maybe that was one lucky thing about this trip. He wouldn't have to write to anyone when he left. There really was something good about every situation, if a guy looked at it the right way. It just seemed that some kinds of luck were better than others. And this kind didn't feel that great.

It was not a good sign the next morning when Bernard met Lucky at the corner a block from the school and called out, "Don't go down there. He's waiting for you!"

"Me? You're the one who smarted off to him. Why didn't he just clobber you on the bus?"

"I didn't ride the bus. Mom drove me. I had her drop me off up here. I told her I was going to meet you and Michael."

"Michael doesn't go to this school. You know that."

"Well, yeah. But she doesn't."

Good ol' Bernard. "So how do you know Bunch is waiting for me?"

"Mom drove past the school. I saw the crowd—and big Bunch right in the middle. Everyone's waiting for the fight. What we've got to do is wait up here and then go in late."

"Maybe Bunch will keep waiting, even after the bell rings."

"No way. He doesn't know you can do that."

"What?"

"Never mind. You have to understand a guy like Bunch."

Lucky doubted he could do that. He was having enough trouble trying to figure out Bernard. "But I don't want to go in late," Lucky said.

"See. You're like Bunch. It's not that big a deal. I do it all the time. Anyway, so what if you get a tardy mark? You're leaving in a couple of weeks. By the way, do you ever get any grades?"

"Not very often. Usually I just—"

"Then what difference does it make?"

Bernard had a point, of course. But Lucky wasn't one who liked to break rules. Of course, he wasn't one who liked to die at the age of eleven either. So he decided to take his chances with a tardy.

And it worked.

Sort of.

It delayed doomsday until that afternoon. After school Lucky and Bernard tried to cross Bunch up by going out the back door again. They figured he would expect a switch, but they guessed wrong about his thinking (or that he thought), and they walked right into him again.

The only thing that made sense to Lucky this time was to assume that Bunch would go for Bernard first—since he was the mouthy one. Bernard, however, pointed off to the right and said, "Hey, Bunch, look at that."

And Bunch looked.

Bernard took off to the left and got away. Lucky couldn't believe anyone would fall for something that stupid. But he figured it was worth another try. "Hey, Bunch, look at that," Lucky said, and he pointed the same direction.

Bunch smiled. His giant teeth, surprisingly white, appeared. Maybe he had been gnawing on bones to keep them clean. "No way," he said. "How stupid do you think I am?"

Lucky knew the right answer this time. "I don't think you're stupid at all, Bunch."

"Then come and play with me. We're going to play some more basketball today."

"Okay, don't look over there. Bernard warned you once, and I'm warning you again, but the guy who threw the snowball at you is waiting to get you again."

Bunch couldn't resist. He took a very quick glance, and Lucky broke for it. Bunch had a good angle, though, and he reacted fast enough to cut Lucky off and get in front of him. Lucky threw on the brakes and then retreated toward the doors. "Bunch, listen to me," he pleaded. "I don't want to fight you. I have no reason to fight you."

"If you fought me Friday, you can fight me again today."

"I didn't fight you. Some kid knocked you down."

A crowd was gathering—as usual—and someone shouted, "No way, Bunch. I saw him push you, and then he jumped on you while you were down."

"Yeah, we saw it," other kids yelled. They were all laughing, as though they were part of a wonderful joke.

Lucky had a sudden vision of these kids visiting the dog pound to watch little stray puppies being put to death.

"Bunch, could we just talk for a few minutes?" Lucky asked. He was moving back, one careful step at a time.

Bunch moved forward. He shook his head and mumbled, "No way. You hurt me."

"Not really. It was all a mistake and a misunderstanding. I really think you and I could be good friends if you'd just give me a chance to—"

Bunch lunged, and Lucky took off, spinning and running for the doors. He got there ahead of Bunch. But a boy was in his way. Lucky grabbed for the door handle. He fought his way around the boy and had the door halfway open when Bunch arrived. Lucky saw Bunch reach for him, and he ducked.

Bunch passed right over Lucky and crashed into the end of the open door. His forehead slammed against the door with another *thonk*. Then he slumped down on top of Lucky.

To save himself from being crushed, Lucky rolled out from under the weight and let the big guy crash to the pavement. At that second, someone screamed, "He did it again! He knocked him out!"

Someone else yelled, "Bunch is dead. You'd better run, Lucky."

Dead? He wasn't dead. His face looked blank but that was only normal. Lucky watched his chest rise and fall. By then, everyone was pushing Lucky away. Then suddenly he found himself running— around the school and most of the way home.

He was almost back to the RV before he told himself he should have stuck around and talked to the principal, or done something other than run again. Chances were, Tuesday would follow Monday, and Bunch, just as surely, would be back again. Waiting.

# CHAPTER 5

When Lucky got to the RV, he was surprised to find Bernard waiting for him.

"Oh, thank goodness," Bernard said. "I've been so worried about you."

"Yeah, right."

"No, really. Did he hurt you at all, or did you get away from him?"

"He ran into a door and knocked himself out."

"All right!" Bernard cheered. He held his hand up for a high five.

Lucky was in no mood for celebrating, though. "Bernard, he's going to get me one of these days. What am I going to do?"

"I don't know, Lucky. It's too bad you ever got him mad at you in the first place."

Oh, brother. Bernard was no help. Lucky wished

the guy would clear out. "Do you need to call your mother?" he asked.

"No. She's picking me up here at 4:30."

That was another hour. Lucky thought about telling him to walk home, but he didn't do it. He got out his key and let Bernard come in. Then Lucky took off his coat and turned on the propane heater. He really wanted to think his situation through. With Bernard around, though, it would be tough.

"What is it with the kids in this school?" Lucky asked. "Bunch runs into a door, and the first thing kids start yelling is that I knocked him out. Do they want me to get killed or something?"

"Hey, Bunch won't kill you. He's never killed anybody. I can think of only one kid who even had to go to the hospital. And it was just for a few stitches or a broken bone or something like that."

"Oh, great." Lucky walked over and sat down on his bed. "Bernard, how do I get Bunch to understand that I don't want to fight him?"

"Well, there's a simple answer. You can't. Bunch just doesn't understand things like that."

"So I have to go to the hospital for stitches or a broken skull before he stops?"

"Well, that might help some. Since you've knocked him out twice, though, he might not think stitches are enough."

Lucky threw his hands in the air, as if to say, "I give up," and then lay back on his bed. "I don't believe that, Bernard. Deep down, Bunch is just like everybody else. He's probably a good guy. Everybody—"

"Lucky, no way. Bunch doesn't have anything like that."

"Like what?"

"Like a deep-down. He doesn't have, you know, like feelings."

"Bernard, he's a human being. Everyone has—"

"Are you sure?"

"Yeah, I'm sure." Lucky suddenly sat up again. "And I'll tell you what else. He'll listen to reason. I really believe that. If I can talk to him alone and explain how this all happened—without everyone screaming for him to punch me—I'll bet we end up friends."

Bernard was nodding. He seemed to be convinced. And he considered for some time before he said, "That kid Bunch beat up got those kind of stitches that dissolve after a while so they're easier to pull out. That's probably the best way to go."

Time to lie down again.

But Lucky was resolved. Maybe Bunch had never been treated like a human being. Maybe that's what he was looking for—just one person to respect him.

"Lucky, I do know what you can do." Bernard walked over and looked down on Lucky. "I can teach you how to defend yourself."

"No way. I'm not going to use karate. If I try to fight the guy, he'll knock my head off."

"I'm not talking about fighting. I'm talking about defending yourself. Karate's not for hurting people; it's for keeping people from hurting you. It's like very spiritual and everything. Our instructor is always talking about stuff like that."

Lucky sat up. "Are you sure?"

"Of course. You can talk all you want, but when Bunch starts swinging, wouldn't you like to know how to block his arm?"

"Yeah, I guess."

"All right. Stand up. Let me show you a couple of things."

Lucky was not at all sure about this. Bernard didn't show a lot of signs of being spiritual—and his main technique seemed to be the old duck and run, the same as Lucky. Still, a little self-protection might not be a bad idea.

"Okay," Bernard said, and he suddenly struck a pose with his feet set, his body bent forward, and his arms cocked and ready. His fingers were curled under with his thumbs tucked in. "The first thing to do is to take your stance, and sometimes that scares a guy off. If it doesn't, use the *kiai*." At that point Bernard let out a deafening howl and thrust his hand at Lucky's chest.

Lucky stepped back, hit his bed with his foot, and stumbled down onto the bed. "Okay. Okay. Not so loud."

"It has to be loud. That's the point. Sometimes just the *kiai* itself—that's the yell—will scare off an attacker. Try it."

So Lucky let out a scream, as loud and fierce as he could come up with.

Bernard laughed. "That wouldn't scare my little sister. Don't just scream. Get some gut into it. Really let out a howl."

Lucky tried again, giving a lower, wilder sort of sound.

"Yeah, well, that's not bad," Bernard said.

"Do you think it would stop Bunch?"

"Not a chance, Lucky."

"Then why did you—"

"I'm just saying that's the first thing you try."

"Okay. What next?"

"Well, let's say he swings at you like this." Bernard swung at Lucky, slow motion. "He's pretty slow. You see his shoulder move, and you pop your arm up, like this." Bernard threw his arm up in a circular motion, ending in front of his face.

Lucky tried it. Bernard helped him adjust the motion a little, and then Lucky practiced a few times. "Okay, good," Bernard said. "Now let's try it. I'll take a slow swing the first time. You block it."

It worked!

Lucky liked this. They tried it several times, and Lucky caught Bernard's oncoming arm every time. Maybe Bernard would turn out to be a helpful friend after all.

"Okay. A little faster. Bunch is slow, but not that slow."

Suddenly the arm was coming and Lucky was late. He thrust up his forearm. He managed to catch Bernard's swing, but the force drove Lucky's arm back. Wham! Lucky hit himself right in the nose. It was exactly what Lucky's dad had predicted.

"Oh, sorry about that!" Bernard said.

Lucky held his nose with his hands. Something begin to ooze between his fingers.

"Oh, man, we seem to have bloodied your nose a little," Bernard said.

Lucky could have figured that one out by himself. He went to the bathroom for a washcloth. Bernard followed. For the next little while, Lucky didn't have much to say.

"You'd better take it easy," Bernard told him. "Why don't you lie down."

That was the best idea Bernard had come up with, ever. And Lucky took the advice. He did say, "Bernard, I think running from Bunch might be better, if it comes to that."

"Well, yeah. That's my theory. But one of these times you might not have a door you can run to."

It was not a good thought.

"We can keep working on your technique, Lucky. You'll get better. Remember, you always have me. If we get cornered, maybe the two of us can fight him off together. I've already had four karate lessons, so I'm getting pretty good."

Right. That's just what Lucky needed: a karate "expert" who had taken four lessons. Lucky shut his eyes and tried to think what he could do if Bunch was waiting for him again in the morning. Just then someone knocked on the door. Bernard whispered, "It must be Bunch." He ran into the bathroom and locked the door.

So much for fighting by Lucky's side!

Lucky thought about hiding under Dad's bed, but he got control of himself enough to peek out the window. The guy outside wasn't Bunch at all. It was Michael.

So Lucky went to the door.

"I need to talk to you," Michael said. He climbed up the step and into the RV.

Lucky stepped aside and let him in, then shut the door to keep the cold air out. He was still holding a washcloth to his nose. Michael didn't even bother to ask about that.

"Look, Lucky," Michael said, "this whole thing with Bunch has got to stop."

"I know."

About then Bernard came out of the bathroom. "Hey, Michael, nice to see you," he said.

Michael took a long look at Bernard and asked, "Who are you?"

"Bernard Pliney. Don't you remember me? I guess I've probably changed a lot since last year. I go to—"

Michael turned away and spoke to Lucky. "My brothers came home talking about how you've been fighting Bunch again."

"Well, it's not true. I—"

"How do you get involved with people like that, Lucky?"

"Involved? I'm not involved. He wants to kill me. Is that—"

"I'm tired of you embarrassing us. I go to school, and everyone wants to know who are the people living in our driveway. And who's the kid fighting with Bunch every day."

"Yes, that would be embarrassing," Bernard said somewhere in the background.

Lucky shot him a dirty look, or at least tried to, with his face mostly covered. He could see how long Bernard's loyalty lasted under pressure.

Michael paid no attention to Bernard. "You don't have to fight Bunch if you refuse to have anything to do with him."

"Michael, he waits for me after school, and I—"

"That's true," Bernard said. "Lucky has tried to—"

"Just don't let it happen again," Michael pronounced, with a finger pointing right between Lucky's eyes. "I don't want to have to ask my father to have you leave."

Michael turned and left.

Lucky shook his head. "What does he expect me to—"

"Boy oh boy," Bernard said, "I had no idea Michael could be so rude. He wouldn't even let me finish a sentence without interrupting me."

Lucky went back to his bed again. He really needed some rest. Trying to communicate with

Bunch would not be easy, though it couldn't be any worse than dealing with Michael—or *Bern*-erd! In time—what seemed a very long time—Mrs. Pliney arrived.

After that, Lucky spent a long evening thinking what he should do. He decided only one approach made sense. The next morning, when he went to school, he would wait by the buses, find Bunch, and tell him how sorry he was for everything. He would talk things out and make it clear to Bunch that everyone was forcing them into something that neither one of them wanted.

Everyone in town believed that wouldn't work, yet had anyone ever really tried? They'd all made up their minds about the guy, and it just wasn't fair. Lucky would show these kids who Bunch really was. He'd appeal to his good side, just the way Dad had told him to do.

It sounded good.

Yet, as Lucky stood in front of the school the next morning and buses started to pull up, his knees were dancing up and down as though he were dying from frostbite. At the same time his hands were sweating inside his coat pockets. Maybe he did have a few doubts about his approach.

But he didn't back away.

The big moment finally came. Bus 14.

The first kid who got off took one look at Lucky and said, "You got to be kidding!" He scooted off to the side and yelled to someone, "The new kid is waiting for Bunch! This is going to be good."

Lucky saw the word spread through the bus, and every kid who got off cleared out of the way fast. No one left, though. A circle formed. Finally, from the very back of the bus, came Bunch.

He stood on the top step, like King Kong staring down from the Empire State Building. His shoulders were hunched high . . . but something was strange. One arm was under his coat, and the sleeve was hanging loose. Bunch came down the stairs awkwardly, holding the rail with his good hand. Lucky could now see that Bunch had a huge knot on his forehead, and both his eyes were black. He looked pale.

In the crowd, someone whispered, "That's the kid who broke Bunch's arm."

Lucky couldn't believe it. "What happened to your arm?" Lucky asked.

Bunch was walking on by. "You broke my wrist" was all he said.

Lucky felt sick. Broke his wrist? How could that—

"My big brother is going to kill you."

Big brother? The funny feeling in Lucky's stom-

ach was turning into nausea. He hurried over to
Bunch. "You must have reached for me and hit the
door with your hand or something. Or maybe you
hurt it when you fell. All I did was duck."

"He's coming over this afternoon," Bunch said.
"I'd hurt you, but the doctor said I can't. My brother
is going to do it for me."

Someone in the crowd said, "He's going to have
Crunch take care of him."

Crunch?

"Listen to me, Bunch." Lucky followed after the
big guy as he trudged toward the school, the crowd
moving with him. "I never intended for all this to
happen. I—"

"My brother says he's going to give you two
concussions and one broken arm. The same as you
gave me. That's fair. He'd do more, but he's bigger
than you."

"But . . . but . . . wait a minute." Two concussions? On one day? "Bunch, a guy can't—"

Bunch just walked into the building.

Lucky was left standing on the front stairs, saying, "Two concussions. You can't give a guy two
concussions."

From nowhere, up stepped Bernard. "Maybe
one in the front and one in the back," he said. "That
might work."

Lucky nodded. He had to admit it. That probably would work. Leave it to Bernard. He could
always think of an answer.

"Lucky," Bernard said, "we're going to have to
do a crash course on the old karate. Crunch is a lot
bigger than his little brother."

Lucky couldn't even imagine that.

# CHAPTER 6

*L*ucky went to class. That morning he learned more about the Civil War. For the first time in his life, he really wondered why the North and South couldn't have just talked things over. "I'll tell you what," he heard Lincoln saying, "slavery is really not a good thing. You've got to admit that. Then again, I guess the states do have rights. I mean, sure. We could throw in a few more of those. Now come on, Jeff, why don't we just settle this and not shoot each other, okay?"

Then he heard Jefferson Davis saying, "Well, sure, Abe, that sounds fair enough. I mean, you guys are our brothers and all. We never really wanted to leave the Union in the first place."

Really, it just made so much more sense. How did these things get started? Maybe there were too many Bernards around, smarting off and then jumping out of the way. Or maybe there were too many spectators saying, "Yeah, ride in there, cavalry. I want to watch this. This should be good."

Lucky should have kept all this to himself, though. When he told the teacher that he thought the North and South should have held a meeting and settled things, Ms. Parlucci said, "Oh, Lucky, I wish things were that simple."

Lucky asked, "Aren't they?"

Everyone laughed, including Ms. Parlucci.

Then, just when Lucky was going to tell them what Lincoln could have said, a girl walked into the room with a green slip of paper and handed it to Ms. Parlucci.

"Lucky, this is for you," she said. "You're supposed to go to the principal's office."

Some boy in the back said, "Uh oh. Lucky gets it now. He never should have beat up on Bunch."

Lucky turned and said, "Are you nuts? I'd have a better chance against the South."

Of course, he meant the southern army, but Ms. Parlucci had no idea what he was talking about. "That's enough, Lucky," she said. "Go down to the office."

So Lucky went. He was pretty sure now how wars got started. Someone probably didn't really do anything, but everyone stood around and said he did, and even those who knew better didn't say anything. The world was starting to make sense.

But maybe this would be different. Maybe the principal would listen. Maybe it was good that he was finally getting to tell the whole truth and straighten this thing out.

Once he was in Dr. Kinski's office, explaining, he began to feel much better. She listened and nodded and seemed to be very understanding. With that kind of encouragement, Lucky told every detail, and he ended with his big pitch: "So you can see what happened. It was all a big misunderstanding. I never threw a punch. I never did one thing wrong. All the injuries were accidents. And I've been thinking, it's sort of like war. I think if people would sit down and talk out their differences, wars would never even happen. It makes sense. If I could spend a half hour with Bunch, we could reach an understanding and come out friends."

That's the only time Dr. Kinski smiled.

She leaned forward, and she looked very pleased. She was a solid-looking woman, with a strong, straight look in her dark eyes, and yet she had a soft, friendly sort of smile. She seemed someone Lucky could rely on. "Well, Lucky," she said, "I'm glad I've heard your side of it. I've already talked to Darwin, so I've heard his version."

"Who?"

"Darwin Bunch."

"Oh. I didn't know he had a first name."

"Of course he has a first name. I think part of the problem is the way kids dehumanize him by talking about him as though he were a *thing*."

Lucky was thrilled. "Exactly. That's what I think too. I asked him what his first name was. He wouldn't tell me at the time. Now I can start calling him Darwin, and—"

"No, no, no. Don't do that."

"What?"

"He hates that name. He beats up on anyone who calls him that."

"But—"

"Look, Lucky, you aren't going to be here long, right?"

"That's right."

"Okay. I've warned Bunch . . . or, Darwin . . . to stay away from you, and he's promised he will. I want you to do the same. For heaven's sake, don't talk to him. We've never had much luck with that."

"But I hate to leave here without—"

"Lucky, trust me. Bunch has been talked to by counselors, psychologists, police officers, and . . . you name it. He's not going to listen to you."

"Well, okay," Lucky said. He told himself that

somehow, before he left this town, he would straighten things out with Bunch, no matter what Dr. Kinski said. For the moment, however, he had a bigger problem. "One thing I do need to mention, Dr. Kinski," he said carefully. "Darwin's brother says he's going to give me two concussions and a broken arm."

"Don't worry about that. I've talked to the family. I've warned them that no reprisals are going to happen. The older boy will be in a juvenile lock-up again if he bothers you."

Again? Lucky finally nodded. "All right, I guess." Lucky stood up. "Thanks a lot for—"

"Wait just a minute, young man. I'm not quite finished here. Fighting is very serious business. I've got to have your commitment that you won't be in any more fights while you're at our school."

"Huh . . . " Lucky was stunned. He finally got enough voice to say, "I told you what happened. I haven't been in any fights. I tried to *stop* Bunch from fighting."

"That's what you say. However, there are always two sides to every story."

Lucky was staring. Dr. Kinski actually glanced away. It was the first little hint of weakness. Suddenly Lucky had to wonder about this woman.

"Every word I told you is true," Lucky said.

"Take a look at me, Dr. Kinski. Do you really think I'd try to fight a guy as big as . . . Darwin? Do you really think I broke his hand or slugged him so hard I knocked him down?"

"I don't know what exactly happened. All I know is that the Bunch family has threatened to sue you and the school, and I've talked them out of it. I promised that you wouldn't hurt him again."

Lucky was developing a serious case of owl eyes. "Dr. Kinski, you can't be serious."

"Long after you're gone, Lucky, I'll be dealing with that Bunch bunch. I didn't see any of this business, and I have no way of proving what happened. So the best thing is to warn both of you to stay away from each other and leave it at that." Then, looking straight at her desk, and in a voice that had lost all conviction, she added, "If you get in trouble again during the time you're here, I'll have to suspend you."

Lucky still wasn't moving. How could this be happening? He had told her the truth, the whole truth. What other side to the story was there?

"Dr. Kinski, could you call in Bernard Pliney and ask him? He was there the day all this started."

"That isn't necessary, Lucky. You have agreed to stay away from Darwin, and he's agreed to stay away from you. The only thing I'm asking is that you behave properly from now on." The strong voice was back. Then it tapered off into a weak, "If you were staying any longer I would ask your father to come in, but I'll just leave this whole thing with a reprimand for right now."

"Why not call in Bernard?"

"There's nothing more to accomplish, Lucky."

"But there is. You're saying I lied, and I didn't."

"I'm not saying you lied. I'm saying you told a different story from the one Darwin told, and in these kinds of cases, each side always does."

"Well, then get some witnesses."

Dr. Kinski suddenly stood up. "I don't need witnesses. This isn't a court case. Just go back to your room now."

"Bernard can—"

Dr. Kinski's voice suddenly jumped to a higher pitch. "Bernard wouldn't know the truth if it stuck to his fingers," she almost shouted.

Lucky had to admit that she had a point.

Dr. Kinski composed herself and added, "But don't ever say that I said that."

Lucky suddenly saw the truth—the whole truth and nothing but the truth. What good would witnesses do? She was right about Bernard, and the kids who saw everything were going around the school saying Lucky had punched Bunch. So Lucky gave up and went back to class. But his eyes stayed wide open all that morning, and he kept staring at the new world he was seeing.

Could it be possible that truth didn't win out? His own dad had told him that it did. Was he planning to tell Lucky the real truth when he got a little older? Or did everyone else already know this stuff? Was this another one of those Santa Claus kind of deals? Lucky was still kind of miffed over that one.

He could see it now: "Son, I think you're old enough now to learn that there really isn't such a thing as honesty. It's just one guy's story against another. Don't worry, you can still believe in the spirit of honesty. Just don't tell any little kids, okay?"

What kind of world was this?

Lucky thought about the whole thing all morning. He felt as though someone had bonked him over the head. Maybe this was concussion number one.

At lunch, Lucky still couldn't get his thoughts back to normal. He was sitting at a table by himself staring at his ugly food when Bernard's voice crashed into his consciousness. "I heard Kinski called you on the carpet," Bernard said and laughed in a long series of squeaks. "What did she say?"

Lucky stared at the kid for several seconds—

until he quit laughing. Then he said, "She told me to stay away from Darwin."

"Oooh, Lucky, don't ever say that name. He might hear you."

"She told me to stay away from him."

"That's good advice, Lucky. One of these times he's really going to hurt you. And your karate has a long way to go."

"Bernard, listen to me. She told me there are two sides to every story. She didn't believe what I told her."

"Yeah, well, it doesn't really matter. She won't do anything, anyway. The big thing is, you've got to watch out for Crunch."

Lucky was suddenly reminded that he could at least be relieved about one thing. "No, that's taken care of. Dr. Kinski talked to the Bunches, and Crunch won't bother me. He's been in a lock-up before, and if he gets in trouble again, he'll—"

"Lucky, you're kidding. You didn't believe that, did you?"

"Believe Dr. Kinski?"

"Yeah. Or the Bunches. Crunch is going to get you. He'll just do it away from school. Just when you least expect it, he'll be there . . . waiting for you. It's like one of those movies where—"

Lucky got up and walked away. He left his food,

and he left Bernard. He had heard enough. The world had no right to go around pretending to be one thing and then suddenly turning out to be something else. He knew Dr. Kinski didn't believe him, but it hadn't occurred to him that he shouldn't believe her. This was amazing. Bernard's dad must have already talked to him. Bernard already understood this stuff. How come Lucky was always the last to know?

All week long Lucky waited. Somewhere out there, the Truth was waiting, and his name was Crunch. He was waiting with two concussions and a broken bone. He was lurking in the dark somewhere, hidden behind Dr. Kinski's friendly smile, and hidden behind Dad's fatherly advice.

Lucky told his dad all about his conversation with Dr. Kinski, and mostly Dad disagreed with her. He told Lucky, "Well, she may be too busy to get to the bottom of this, but that doesn't change the truth. The important thing is, you know what that truth is."

"How does that help anything if no one trusts anyone else?"

"I'm not saying truth wins all the battles," was all Lucky's father could come up with. "But I still think it wins out in the long run. I don't want you to lose your trust in that."

Despite his feelings, Lucky went about his business as though the world hadn't turned upside down. Ms. Parlucci carried on quite normally—acting as though the Civil War made perfect sense. And the kids at school were doing the usual stuff. No one came up to him and said, "So did your dad tell you about truth yet?"

They also seemed to forget about the whole Bunch/Lucky affair. Maybe that was old news now that no one had been bodily damaged for a couple of days. Talk turned to the Celtics or television or athletic shoes. And all this time Lucky walked around with wide eyes . . . knowing, and waiting for Crunch.

Then Friday afternoon came.

Lucky knew something was up when a crowd followed him up the street—twenty steps back. He asked them what was going on, but they wouldn't talk.

Bernard came running up to catch Lucky. "Lucky, Lucky, don't go home that way. He's up there. The word is out."

"Good," Lucky said.

"What?"

"Good. I need to talk to him."

"Lucky, you might as well talk to a pipe bomb."

"It's my last chance."

"Run, Lucky! It's your only chance. You'll never be able to block his punches."

"I'm not running," Lucky said. "I'm going to *talk* to him."

Lucky told himself he was giving truth and reason one last try. If it didn't work, then he would give up and become just like Bernard.

What a thought!

# CHAPTER 7

Lucky walked straight up to the guy and said, "Are you Crunch?"

It was a little like walking up to Mount St. Helens and asking, "Are you the volcano?" The only logical answer to either question was "Do you see any other mountains around here?"

That's not what Crunch said. Crunch said, "Don't ever call me that again."

"Oh, I'm sorry," Lucky said. "It's the only name I've heard. What is your first name?"

Crunch and a couple of his buddies were standing in the middle of the sidewalk, on a corner, apparently awaiting Lucky's arrival. The crowd was coming in a little closer now, circling all the way around. Crunch looked very much like his brother, in the way one sand dune looks like another. He had nostrils, but nothing much that anyone could call a nose, and his eyes looked like holes in the sand.

Crunch was taken off guard by Lucky's strange question. Maybe no one—at least no kid—had ever asked to know his name. "Shut up," Crunch mumbled, and he bought himself some time to think. Either that, or he forgot what he was doing. In any case, Crunch stood in a state of... absence ... for a time. Finally he said, "I'm looking for you." That seemed to mean, "What are you walking up to me for? You're supposed to be clearing out." Lucky had learned to read between the lines with the Bunch boys.

"I know. I was looking for you too. I wanted to talk things over. You know, this whole thing has been a huge misunderstanding."

"Oh, yeah?" Crunch said—which seemed to mean, "Don't contradict me." Suddenly a paw the size of a catcher's mitt struck Lucky right in the chest. Lucky shot backward and landed on his rear, at the feet of all his fans. They cheered and then made little chirping, gurgling noises, like buzzards happy that a meal was about to be served.

Lucky tried to think why he hadn't used his karate blocking motion. But this Crunch guy was quicker than his brother—or Bernard.

Lucky didn't jump up and run, though. He got

up, slowly, and then said, "This isn't going to solve anything. Can't we just talk things out and—"

*Wham!*

Lucky went down again. This time he took a little more time getting up. He was feeling dizzy. He tried to remember that karate stance he had learned. He even thought about doing one of those screams, but he didn't consider it long. His only chance was to make peace.

"See, you can beat me up, easy. That doesn't prove anything. If we could just sit down together and I could explain how this whole misunderstanding began, then I'm sure—"

*Wham!!*

This time when Lucky hit the ground, he saw a few dancing lights before his eyes. He was beginning to lose interest in chatting with Crunch this way. He didn't know what else to do but get up. He made a quick decision not to say anything and see whether communication wouldn't improve. But silence didn't work either.

*Wham!!!*

Lucky stayed down this time. He had an idea. "Oh, wow," he whispered, "I think I've got a concussion." He had no more than said it when he realized his mistake. He quickly added, "Maybe two."

It was too late. Crunch pulled him to his feet and then, *Wham!!!!*

Lucky knew what to do this time. "Oh, no!" he moaned. "My arm is broken. Two concussions and a broken arm."

Some smart aleck was saying, "No way. He's faking it."

However, when Lucky opened his eyes, Crunch was gone. That was probably because someone had yelled, "Here comes a teacher."

When the world stopped rotating counterclockwise, Lucky sat up. Most of the kids were gone, and a large man with a droopy mustache was repeating, "Are you okay?"

From somewhere Bernard appeared again—although he had vanished during the confrontation. He was leaning over the teacher's shoulder, saying, "Good plan, Lucky. Faking injuries was smart."

"I thought you were going to help me," Lucky moaned.

"Yeah, well, I did tell you to run. Remember?"

By now Lucky was starting to wonder whether his injuries were fakes after all. Sure, his arm was okay. But he thought he felt at least two concussions inside there somewhere.

The teacher helped Lucky to his feet, and for a moment Lucky wobbled like a newborn colt. All the same, the man's only response was to say, "Maybe you'd better head home."

Lucky had been expecting him to offer an ambulance, or at least a ride in his car.

"Don't worry, I'll take him home," Bernard said, and he laughed. "He's not really hurt."

That's when the teacher delivered the hardest blow Lucky had taken all day—even more than being Crunched. The guy pointed a huge, hairy finger into Lucky's face and said, "You're just lucky you didn't get hurt. You ought to know better than to get in a fight with a Bunch."

"But I didn't—"

"I'm afraid I'll have to report this to Dr. Kinski. If you think you're roughed up now, just wait until she finishes with you."

Lucky's mouth fell open. With his droopy eyes and wide-open mouth, he stood there looking like a fish as the teacher trudged back to the school.

Bernard had the right answer, though. "Lucky, don't sweat it. If you get kicked out of school, that could actually save your life. When Crunch finds out your arm isn't broken, he'll be back, you know." He patted Lucky on the shoulder, as though he really felt some compassion. Then he added, "I tried to tell you not to talk to him. I knew that wouldn't work."

"Bernard, I still think we could talk things out if everyone wouldn't crowd around and start cheering him on."

Bernard laughed a little and shook his had. "You really believe that, don't you?"

"Yes, I do."

"Well, little guy, all I can say is, you've got a lot to learn about this old world."

Lucky couldn't believe this. "Bernard," he said, "leave me alone, okay? Just stay away from me."

Lucky walked away. He wasn't too steady on his feet, but he knew that he wanted to get far away from Bernard.

"So is that the thanks I get for helping you?" Bernard asked.

Lucky didn't look back. He had to concentrate on more basic things—like putting one foot in front of the other.

When Lucky got home, he rested. He was soon convinced that aside from some aches and pains, he wasn't hurt seriously. He had taken some bad blows in the past—on his skateboard and in flag football—and he had always gotten back up. He would survive this time too.

It was the injustice of the whole situation that was driving him crazy. By now Dr. Kinski had probably gotten the report that he was fighting again. It was maddening.

After his father came home, Lucky poured out the whole story. He knew one thing for sure: Dad could get things straightened out.

And his dad said just the right thing. He patted Lucky on the shoulder (which sent jarring pains down Lucky's spine) and said, "Lucky, I admire you for what you tried to do. Don't worry, we'll get this all taken care of. I'll call the principal on Monday. I'm sure she'll listen to reason. We'll get these Bunch kids stopped if we have to call the police."

Suddenly the world was okay again. It was a great moment. Good ol' Dad would come through for him. Maybe the world was messed up, but Dad was still on his side.

Then his dear father said, "Lucky, I do have to say this: you've got to become a little more realistic. You always think you can go around solving everyone's problems. That's not bad in some ways, but you can see what it got you this time."

*Wham!!!!!*

"Dad, I only tried to talk to people. I didn't hit anyone, or threaten anyone, or . . . anything."

"I know that. I'm just saying that at your size you don't have to be the one to stand up to all the big guys in this world."

"Who stops them then? Even the principal is afraid of them. They can mash people, and then lie, and she's afraid to tell them that they're liars."

"Well, these kinds of things are complicated, and it's not easy to sort them out."

Then Dad got busy making dinner. He told Lucky to rest. Lucky tried, but he wasn't very relaxed. He just wasn't sure his dad really understood.

Complicated? What was so complicated?

Still, Lucky was thinking that on Monday maybe some justice would be done, once Dad told Dr. Kinski a thing or two. Dad could get tough when he was standing up for things he believed in. He was a nice man, but when someone tried to give Lucky a bad deal, he could get awfully . . .

"Lucky," Dad said, "there's one more thing I want to say about all this."

Lucky waited. He hoped his dad would say, "Right is right. And wrong is wrong. We aren't going to stop fighting until we make sure justice is done."

That's not what he said.

Mr. Ladd paused for quite some time, choosing his words carefully. "You have to remember that sometimes life isn't fair. I'm afraid big guys do take advantage of little guys. And people with power don't always use it right. It's not a very pleasant thing to admit. Part of growing up is understanding that."

"But Dad, you always said to stand up for things that are right."

"Sure. I still say that. But that doesn't mean that you'll always win. I'm afraid that 'right' takes a pretty hard beating in this world sometimes. I still say truth wins out in the long run. Sometimes, though, that 'long run' runs pretty long."

So this was it. The Santa Claus talk.

On Monday Dr. Kinski would probably beat him up herself, or maybe help Bunch do it. And Dad would watch the whole thing, then say, "Well, Lucky, I told you life isn't always fair."

Some world.

His father was approaching Lucky's bed now. He was probably going to pound on Lucky's bruises, or maybe try a little more verbal abuse. "Just remember what I told you first. I do admire you. I just worry that you might get hurt."

"Or that I might get some crazy idea in my head that life should be fair."

Dad chuckled in that big, rumbling voice of his. "Hey, Lucky, I think life should be fair. I also know that sometimes it isn't."

"Like when your principal says you're a liar when you're not, and then you get beat up by a guy the size of Mount Everest, and you go home and tell your dad, and he says that things are complicated? Would that be an example?"

"Well, yeah, that would be pretty good. But let's say you got teased at church for living in an RV, and the kid who lives in the house where you're parked keeps treating you like you're some sort of lowlife. If you threw in stuff like that, I think your example would be better."

"Well, what if this same kid had great big teeth that stuck way out, and he was just a little shrimp? Wouldn't that be an even better example?"

All this time Lucky had never really looked at his dad. When he heard nothing for a long time, he peeked. His father was grinning. Once Dad got the eye contact, he said, "On the other hand, if that same kid were destined for big things in his life, and if he got to travel all around with his terrific father and learn all kinds of fantastic stuff, and if he happened to be the greatest kid there ever was, and if he were the luckiest kid anyone ever knew, then that, my friend, would ruin the example."

"Yeah, I'm lucky all right," Lucky said, and he rolled over. He only did that, though, because he didn't want his dad to see that he was starting to smile. And he didn't want to smile because he didn't want his dad to win this one. Lucky was upset and disgusted, and Dad couldn't just make him laugh the whole thing away.

"If I say you're lucky, you're lucky. That's the rule around here. I'm the boss of deciding luck. And you don't get a vote."

"Cheater," Lucky said. Now he was fighting hard not to laugh.

"That's another rule. You can't call your dear papa any bad names. I can call you anything I want—including lamb chops or lollipop—but you can't call me *nothing*."

It was the lamb chops and the lollipop that got poor Lucky. A little laugh slipped out. His dad laughed a lot—and loud—which made Lucky laugh even more. They continued to laugh until they hurt. Of course, for Lucky, having been Crunched just a little while earlier, it didn't take all that much laughing to cause pain.

# CHAPTER 8

**O**n Saturday the Bunches showed up. Crunch Bunch and plain Bunch—both of them.

Lucky felt them lurking outside before he saw them through the window, and then their shadows came toward the RV and blocked out the light. When he heard thunder, he thought a storm had blown in with them. Actually they had only knocked on the door.

Lucky looked out the window, though only to verify what he already knew. "Dad, it's the Bunches. They're coming after me. Don't open the door."

Dad shook his head as if to say, "Do you think I'm afraid of them? They're just kids."

But Lucky thought he saw some surprise on his dad's face when he opened the door. "Yes?" he said—sort of timidly.

"We were just wondering if Lucky's arm was broken," a soft, deep voice said.

Lucky didn't know those guys were capable of sounding so gentle.

"No, his arm is not broken. He's pretty banged up, though, thanks to you."

"We're sorry about that," the voice said. "I think it was all caused by a misunderstanding."

It had to be the longest word Crunch had spoken in his life, and Lucky knew where he had learned it. He didn't believe a word of this.

"Well, I'm glad you feel that way," Dad said.

Oh, brother. He was buying it.

"Does Lucky want to come out and play?"

Come out and play? Get serious.

Dad turned to Lucky and said, "Son, I think the Bunch brothers want to end this silly feud. Do you want to talk to them?"

"No, no, no," Lucky whispered intensely. "Dad, they're trying to get me again."

"Lucky, you've been wanting to talk to them without a crowd around. This is your chance." Dad walked over to Lucky, who had scrunched himself into the corner, on his bed. Dad was the size of a Bunch, and right now there seemed a very good chance that he was actually one of them.

"They just want to finish what they started, Dad. They still owe me a broken arm."

"Look, you know these guys better than I do, and you may be right. But I wish you'd give them a chance before you make up your mind. I don't want you to come out of this situation as a cynic. You've always had such a good outlook on life."

"What's a cynic?"

"Well, it's a . . . I don't know an exact definition. It's someone who doesn't put much faith in other people."

"I don't know, Dad. I . . . " Lucky was wavering, though, and Dad seemed to see it.

"Just step outside and talk to them. I'll keep the door open, and I'll watch. They won't try anything with me nearby."

That was probably right. Besides, Lucky was the one who kept telling Bernard that the Bunches would listen to reason. He had to give them at least one more chance.

So Lucky got up and walked to the door. When he saw the two hulks waiting, he almost lost his nerve. He had never seen them together, and the total mass dwarfed the door.

"Hi," he said, then slowly climbed down the steps onto the ground and into the shadows of death.

"Wanna play football?" Crunch said. He was crushing a football under his arm, and something in his eyes said that he wished he had hold of Lucky instead.

"Where?" Lucky said. He saw the trap.

"I don't know. Down at the school, I guess. We could get some other guys."

No way. Lucky wasn't walking away with these tanks. "I thought you didn't like me."

Crunch took a slow look at his brother. Both of them smiled, ever so slightly. "We wanna be friends now," Crunch said.

"Why?"

Lucky saw the confusion come into Crunch's eyes. This was no easy question. Then a little light came on, and Crunch said, "Fighting is bad."

Bunch nodded, slowly. "We don't want to fight anymore." The little smile came back. "Someone could get hurt."

Now Lucky had to decide. If he walked away with these guys, he might never walk back. And if he didn't, he would never know what they really wanted.

His father was still standing in the doorway, and he answered the question for Lucky. "Son, I think you'd better not run off right now while you're all banged up. Why don't you fellows just talk a little, and see if you can't work out your differences?"

Lucky nodded. But he wasn't sure what to say. Finally, he looked at Bunch — and carefully avoided his name. "I didn't knock you down that day. A kid was sliding on the snow. He did it — by accident."

Bunch nodded just a bit, and he didn't say anything. His lipless mouth was still curved, just slightly, into the bare suggestion of a smile.

"And I didn't break your arm. You ran into the door. All I did was duck."

Both boys nodded this time. And both of them made the same little smile. Lucky didn't quite know what it meant.

Lucky looked over at Crunch. "And I only came up to you on the street so that I could talk to you and see if we couldn't be friends. I didn't want to fight."

The boys were still nodding, and Crunch said, "We understand now. We want to be friends too. Can you play football tomorrow?"

"Not on Sunday. I go to church on Sunday."

"How about Monday? After school."

"Uh . . . maybe. I'll have to see."

"Okay," Crunch said. His head was still bobbing slowly up and down. "See you Monday." A bigger grin broke out—and teeth the size of razor blades appeared.

Lucky shuddered.

Then the mountains moved away, letting the sunlight return, and Lucky went back into the RV. "They still want to kill me, Dad. I'm sure of it."

Dad sort of shrugged. "Well, maybe. They're kind of hard to read. Then again, who knows? Maybe they aren't very good at expressing their feelings. Maybe they really do want to make things right."

"Why would they? Why would they change from yesterday?"

"Well . . . it's hard to say. Maybe someone talked to them. Or maybe Crunch felt bad after he knocked you around."

"Do you really believe that?"

Dad was looking down at Lucky, but he seemed to lose his confidence. His eyes wandered away— the way Dr. Kinski's had done. "Well, let's say I hope that's what's happening."

Lucky wanted to believe it too. Yet he remembered those ugly little smiles. "I don't think so, Dad. I don't trust them. I think I *am* a cynic."

All weekend Lucky wondered. Something about being a cynic appealed to him. It was like calling himself a man. His whole life he had been the little kid who trusted everyone. Now, though, he had met the Bunches and Michael — and Bernard — and now his dad had told him that a lot of things were "complicated." He wasn't the little kid he had been when he first arrived in Rockbridge.

On Sunday, at church, when Michael acted like a jerk, Lucky was sort of glad. It fit what he was suspecting. Rich kids thought they had the right to look down on everyone else. They were another kind of bully. They weren't to be trusted. A cynic knew better.

Still, there were other factors to consider. Michael's beautiful big sister Emily was just as rich as Michael, and she was nice. She could be faking it, of course, though she didn't seem to be.

And there was still one other possibility — no matter how slight. Maybe the Bunches really did want to play football and be friends. Maybe they had no intention of mangling and maiming him. Maybe that little smile was just their way of showing their satisfaction in being friends.

Naaaahhhhh. It wasn't likely. Being a cynic made more sense.

The only problem was, it wasn't easy to be a cynic with his dad around. After church, he shook 'n' baked some chicken breasts while Lucky tore up a head of lettuce. When Dad finally shoveled a pitchfork load of lettuce into his mouth, he said, "Uhm, uhm. You sure do know how to make a good salad."

"It's all in the way you rip the lettuce," Lucky said, grinning.

"Well, here's the thing I like. A lot of people mess up their salads with all kinds of stuff—red cabbage, green onions, cauliflower, Brussels sprouts, bacon bits, croutons, crab grass, pussy willows, and who knows what else. But not you, Lucky my boy. You make a pure salad. A perfect salad. I expect you to be a great chef when you grow up— much as I am."

"Yeah, but I'll only do salads."

"That's right, Son. Only lettuce salads. But don't ever reveal your secret ingredient. If you do, everyone will start copying it, and you'll be out of a job."

By now Lucky was giggling even though he hadn't been in a very good mood before. "Maybe if someone steals my idea, I could change over to some of those other kinds of lettuce that they have at the store. Like that—"

"Never. Never. None of that leaf lettuce, or Chinese elm—or whatever they call it. With you it will always be pure, regular, spectacular *head* lettuce. Stick with the stuff that made you famous. Dance with the girl that brung ya'. That's what I always say, even though I don't have the slightest idea what that means."

Suddenly, with no warning, Dad cracked off a laugh that must have rumbled through the earth's surface for miles around. Lucky jiggled in his seat, partly from his own laughter and partly from the explosion.

"I owe it all to you, Dad. You taught me to tear up my first head of lettuce when I was only just a little kitchen helper."

"Yes, but you've gone way beyond me now, Son. I can't match what you can do. I just hope you'll always remember me when you hit the big time."

And on and on the silly stuff went. By the time Lucky went to bed that night he had forgotten all about being a cynic. Life inside the Ladd RV was just too good.

But on Monday morning, things turned around quickly. Lucky no more than got inside the door to Ms. Parlucci's class than a girl showed up with another green slip for him, and Lucky was off to Kinski's office again.

"I'm sorry," she said, as soon as Lucky sat down. "Enough is enough. Now you've been in another fight and I'm suspending you. You won't get back into this school until your father comes and meets with me."

"But . . . I —"

"No 'buts' from you, young man. Since you arrived at this school, we've had three fights. I've also suspended Bunch . . . or, I mean, Darwin. I've reported to the junior high that the older brother was involved. I'm not playing favorites here."

"Won't you let me explain how it all —"

"I've heard all I want to hear from you. Now I want the fighting stopped. You're suspended."

Lucky gave up. He stood up and walked out the door. Dr. Kinski had helped him make up his mind. He wanted to find out where all the cynics met and join their club. It was the only place he thought he would ever feel comfortable again.

He walked on home, opened up the door to the RV, checked inside for any Bunches, then locked the door. The cynic in him, now alive and well again, told him that it was just a matter of time before his troubles returned. The day was very long, though, and nothing happened. He was starting to think he would survive another day when the dreaded knock came. Lucky stiffened and listened. The only plan that flashed into his head was slamming his arm against a hard object and then sticking the dangling limb out the window for the satisfaction of all Bunches.

Then another possibility occurred to him. "Who is it?" he yelled.

"Michael," the voice said.

Maybe. It could be a trick. "How do I know that?"

"What?"

No, that was him. A Bunch couldn't make his voice go that high.

So Lucky opened the door. Michael stepped up and into the RV without asking for permission, as usual. He looked angry. "Lucky," he said in that whiny voice of his, "did you ask those Bunch boys to come over here?"

"No."

"They were outside just now. They said you invited them to come over and play football."

"I just told them I might play with them. I didn't tell them to come here."

"You're going to play football with the Bunches? Are you nuts?"

Lucky tried to think whether he was or not. Finally he said, "No, I'm not going to play with them. They really want to break my arm or my head or something. They're just lying about the football."

"Well, I'm glad you've got that much figured out. I had to threaten to call the police to get those guys to leave."

"Hey, don't do me any favors. I'll take care of myself."

Michael looked stunned—and Lucky enjoyed the shock. He was tired of putting up with jerks.

Michael looked at Lucky for several seconds. He was wearing another expensive ski jacket—a different one from the one he had worn before. He usually had a way of angling his head back and looking down his nose, but some of that stiffness seemed gone now. "What's got into you?" he finally said. He seemed mystified. Maybe Lucky had finally talked his language.

"I've become a cynic since I moved here. That's what's happened."

"What's that?"

Lucky had enjoyed his announcement, but this question threatened to blow his cover. He paused, struggled for words, then had to admit, "I don't know exactly. But I'm not 'Mr. Nice Guy' anymore." To his disgust, he did the last thing in the world he wanted to do. For no reason he knew of—except that he had sounded so stupid—he let a little smile creep in around the edges of his mouth. He tried to force it away, but it was too late.

Then Michael smiled.

Lucky felt his lips slipping back away from his

braces, and he tried to fight it. But a little laugh
sneaked out.

Then Michael laughed.

"What are you laughing at?" Lucky demanded,
trying to sound gruff. Another laugh slipped out,
and there was no getting it back.

"You'd better at least look the word up before
you become one," Michael said, and he laughed
again.

Lucky gave up all hope when he said, "I would,
but I don't know how to spell it."

It was a strange moment. Both boys laughed,
but when they finished, neither knew what to say.
Michael mumbled something about being careful
about the Bunches and left.

Lucky was left wondering. Was he friends with
Michael now? Would Michael show up wanting to
play football one of these days? Or would he just
go back to being a jerk again? Michael was no easier
to figure than a Bunch was.

# CHAPTER 9

*T*hat night Lucky's father came home late, and tired. Lucky had heated some spaghetti sauce and had the spaghetti ready to boil. He had even created another one of his now-famous lettuce salads. He figured it wouldn't hurt to soften up his dad a little before he gave him the news about school. It probably wasn't the sort of thing a cynic would do. Lucky didn't have any rules to go by, though, so he wasn't really sure.

"Did you call Dr. Kinski today?" Lucky asked.

"Oh. No. I'm sorry, Lucky. I meant to. I got busy, and I didn't think about it. Did she say anything to you?"

"Yup."

"What?"

"Get out."

"Of school?"

"Yup."

"Oh, no. Hey, I'm sorry I didn't call. I'll call her in the morning."

"She wants you to come in and meet with her. I'm suspended until you do."

"Lucky, that's a real problem. I'm supposed to have a meeting first thing in the morning."

"Okay. Well, I can stay home another day." Lucky rather liked the idea.

"No. I don't want you to do that. I'll have to make a phone call tonight and change the meeting." He was setting out a couple of plates on the table. "Lucky, I hope, wherever we move next, that you'll stay out of . . . "

Trouble. But he didn't say it. "Dad, I already told you. I didn't—"

"I know. Sometimes though . . . well, never mind. I'll go in with you in the morning."

Lucky could tell that his dad was tired. He knew it wasn't any fun to come home to one more problem to straighten out. It's what he had to do all day. Yet Lucky still found himself a little irritated with his dad's attitude.

"The next place we go," Lucky said, "I'll stay out of trouble. I'm going to find the biggest, meanest kid in the school and get to be buddies with him. Then, when someone gets beat up, it won't be me.

And if there's some kid like Bernard around, I'll help beat him up."

"Well, now," Dad said, "don't start talking that way again. I'm sure we can convince Dr. Kinski to let you back in school."

Lucky didn't think that was exactly the grand prize of all solutions. He didn't say that, though. He ate his spaghetti in silence — except for the slurping. After dinner he asked his dad if he could walk down to the public library, which wasn't too far away.

Dad said he didn't mind, and he would do the dishes since Lucky had cooked. So Lucky left, and when he got to the library, he knew just what he wanted. He went to the computer terminal and typed in his subject of interest: *karate.* Bernard wasn't much of a teacher; maybe a book would be more help. Lucky knew he needed some way to save his life for another week or two until he and his dad moved again. No matter what his dad said, Lucky was pretty sure the Bunches had more than football in mind. He also figured that Michael hadn't helped any by threatening to call the police.

Lucky wasn't quite so interested in the defensive parts of karate now. He needed to know some sort of chops or punches that could bring a giant to his knees — or at least stun him long enough for Lucky to make a getaway. He found a large book with lots of pictures of kids taking on other kids, and he found just the punch he thought he needed. It was a blow to the solar plexus—right in the middle of the chest. It was supposed to knock the wind out of a guy.

Lucky liked the idea. He didn't think the punch would do any lasting damage to those big Bunch brothers, yet it might slow one down while he made his escape. Besides, their chests might be within his reach.

So Lucky read. Then he practiced. He left out the shouting part, but a couple of people still gave him strange looks as he crouched and started stabbing away at the air. What did Lucky care, though? Cynics didn't worry about what other people thought. Or at least he didn't think so.

When Lucky got back to the RV, Dad was doing some paperwork at the table. Without really showing a lot of interest, he asked, "Did you find what you were looking for, Lucky?"

"Yup."

"And what was that?"

Lucky had been waiting for this. He wanted to shock his dad. "A book on karate. So I can beat up on Bunch and Crunch."

Dad looked up.

"It might be my only chance." He crouched and cocked his arms in front of his face, and he bent his fingers and thumbs in the way the book had shown how to do.

"Lucky, what is this? What happened to talking things out?"

"I don't believe in any of that stuff anymore. I'm a cynic now."

"Since when? I thought you told me the Bunches might have really meant it when they said they were sorry." Dad actually did look concerned, and Lucky liked that.

"That was before Dr. Kinski kicked me out of school. I found out it doesn't do any good to talk. People don't believe the truth. And liars get away with their lies. That's what the Bunches are. Liars. Stand up and I'll show you how I'm going to wipe them out."

"Lucky, you can't fight those guys."

"That's what you think. I learned a karate punch that will knock the wind right out of them. All I have to do is . . . this." He shot out a short twisting thrust that caught Crunch right in the breastbone and dropped him to the floor. Lucky watched him fall, then said, "Right in the solar plexus. And it's good-bye, big guy."

"Lucky, I can't believe you really want to—"

"Stand up, and I'll show you, if you don't believe me." Lucky liked the rude part—interrupting his dad's sentence. That fit right in with his new image.

Dad did stand up, which Lucky hadn't really expected. Lucky moved forward, set himself in his stance, shouted a mild sort of *kiai,* and punched at his dad's chest. He stopped an inch or two short.

"Go ahead. Give me your best shot. Let's see if it works."

"Dad, I don't want to hurt you. A karate guy never hurts anyone if he can help it. That's part of the whole karate thing."

"Maybe so. We need to check this out, though, so you'll know it will work."

Lucky really didn't like this. "Dad, I don't think so. Sometimes it can break a guy's breastbone."

"Okay. Well, I wouldn't want that. Just show me how you do it again."

Lucky didn't mind doing that. He crouched. This time he gave a vicious scream and fired a shot at . . . but his dad stepped forward and Lucky got him. Hit him with all his strength.

Lucky screamed again—but this time from pain. His wrist had twisted against Dad's chest. Lucky grabbed the wrist and sunk to the floor.

Strangely, his dad was still standing. He didn't even have tears in his eyes. In fact, he bent down and put his arm around Lucky's shoulders. "Lucky, I doubt you can learn karate in a few minutes— and from a book. I also doubt that's the answer to your problem."

"Well, what is then? Those guys are going to kill me, and at my funeral, Dr. Kinski's going to tell everyone that it was all my fault."

Dad tried not to laugh, but he did anyway. Softly though. "No way. I'm going to see her, and we're going to get this thing straightened out once and for all."

Lucky didn't admit it—because it wasn't part of being a cynic—but he liked that. Maybe he couldn't trust in anyone else. But he was pretty sure that he could trust in his dad.

The next morning Lucky and Dad walked to school together, then waited until Dr. Kinski could see them. She was very nice to Mr. Ladd. Lucky knew the real Dr. Kinski, though.

"Sit down, Lucky. Sit down, Mr. Ladd," she said, spreading her smile around. That hard-eye look of hers was gone. "Let me say, first, that Lucky seems to be a very nice boy. I don't think that he's normally a troublemaker. I'm afraid circumstances this week just got a little out of control."

"Yes, I think that's right," Lucky's father said.

"The reason I suspended Lucky, along with Darwin Bunch, was that I wanted to stop the trouble before someone got hurt. Some people just say, 'Boys will be boys,' and overlook this kind of thing. We simply do not tolerate fighting in our school."

"I agree, Dr. Kinski. Believe me, Lucky is not a fighter." He didn't mention Lucky's new interest in karate.

Dr. Kinski set her glasses on her desk, smiled a lovely smile, and said, "Well, then, maybe it's good we nipped this in the bud before something really tragic happened. I'll reinstate Lucky, and he can go back to class. I assume I have your promise that there will be no more fighting."

"Of course," Mr. Ladd said, and that was that.

Everything was all settled. Lucky's father was clearing out, ready to head to his meeting, and Dr. Kinski could check something off her "to do" list for the day. So where was Dad's promise to get all this stuff straightened out?

But Lucky didn't budge from his chair. When his father and the principal seemed to realize that — at about the same time — they both looked at him. "I didn't . . . FIGHT . . . ANYONE," he said slowly and firmly.

"Lucky," Dad said, "I know what you mean, but let's just let this whole thing go now, and you can go back to class."

"Sit down, Mr. Ladd," Dr. Kinski said, and her tone said, "Well, it looks as though I've still got business to take care of here." She sat down too. "Lucky, I tried to explain this to you before." She paused and nodded to Dad, as if to reassure him that she could handle this. "I can't be everywhere in the school. I can't know exactly what happens all the time. When trouble begins, I have to assume that both sides had something to do with it."

"Why?"

"Lucky, I just told you why." Dr. Kinski's voice was losing some of its softness. "The Bunch family is calling me and claiming that you broke their son's wrist and that they might file a lawsuit. Meanwhile, you're telling me you're as innocent as a little lamb. I have no way of knowing who's right. I just have to do what it takes to stop the trouble—lawsuits and all the rest. You can understand that, can't you, Lucky?"

"No."

Dr. Kinski gave up on her smile altogether. "What don't you understand?" she asked.

"Okay. What you're saying is that if someone gets in a fight, both kids always lie. But what if sometimes one guy lies and the other one tells the truth?"

"How am I supposed to decide?" Dr. Kinski asked. Now her patience was gone.

Lucky was very calm. He looked at his dad. "If Dr. Kinski always says, 'I guess both kids are lying,' that means liars come out ahead every time. And guys who tell the truth get called liars." He sat back and folded his arms. "The reason I know that could happen is because it did. Bunch is lying, and I'm not."

Dad seemed to listen to that, but Dr. Kinski said, "That's what he says too." A spark in her eye seemed to say, "Now that time I got you."

"I know. But he's lying when he says he's not lying."

Dr. Kinski was staring now. "Lucky, I'm looking out for everyone. I'm protecting the children of this school. This is not an easy job, you know."

"I know all that. But you'd rather call me a liar than find out the truth."

"There's not time enough in my day to track down who's lying and who's not. And I haven't shown any favoritism. You're just not old enough to understand that."

All of a sudden Mr. Ladd rose up like a giant—bigger than a Bunch. "Wait a minute," he said.

Lucky heard the change. He knew his dad was angry, even though he didn't raise his voice.

"Dr. Kinski, I don't like some of the things you've been telling my son. I've taught him to trust in people and do what he believes is right. So when he tries to stop a fight, he ends up getting kicked out of school for it. The trouble is, Dr. Kinski, you're just as afraid of Bunch as everyone else is—or at least afraid of his parents. You'd rather avoid the truth than deal with it."

"Mr. Ladd, you don't have to deal with all the problems that can come up in a day around here."

"No, I don't. And I don't envy you. But I've never known a more idealistic kid than Lucky, and now he's telling me he's a cynic. I think that's because you're a cynic. You don't trust kids. You assume the worst about them. I think I'll take Lucky with me the rest of the time we're here—before you ruin him altogether." With that, he turned and said, "Come on, Lucky, let's go."

And they left.

Dad walked back to the RV, taking those huge strides of his, and Lucky had to trot just to keep up. All the way up the street Dad kept saying stuff like "Lucky, don't give up on people yet. There are plenty of folks in this world you can trust."

Lucky liked what he was hearing. All his life he had known that his dad was the one person he could rely on for sure. And sure enough, he had finally come through.

As the two approached the RV, Dad said, "I don't want to hear any more talk about being a cynic. I've seen you inspire people with your great attitude. It would be a tragedy for you to change."

Lucky did have the feeling that the cynic thing never had seemed quite natural. He knew he had been hoping all along that it wouldn't work out. Still, he hated to admit to that. So he only said, "Well, I'll have to think about it."

"You do that, Lucky. And you remember all the people you'd be letting down if you decided to have a bad attitude about life. Think about the influence you've had on some of your friends. Do you want to walk away from that? And your poor Mom; she's probably worried sick. You think about that."

It was a good point. Too good. Lucky felt rather ashamed of himself.

But somewhere out there, the Bunches were still waiting. He was pretty sure of that. And something told him there were always Bunches around somewhere. Lucky wasn't quite ready to forget that either.

# CHAPTER 10

Lucky took the train into town with his dad that day, and when they got off downtown, they walked to Dad's insurance office. Lucky waited while Dad met with some people. After the meeting, Dad took Lucky on the subway—the "T"—and they rode to the area where the fire had occurred. They walked around the block and looked at all the buildings that had been destroyed.

Lucky's father didn't say much. He just pointed out all the damage. "An older man died in this one," he said. "They found him on the floor. He tried to crawl to the door. The smoke got to him before he could make it."

When they had made the loop around the block, Dad walked on up the street. Along the way, Lucky saw a world he had never seen up close before. The old apartment houses were run down, with screens torn, even some windows broken and covered with cardboard. And the people who were outside looked beaten down—as though a Bunch had been pounding on them all their lives.

Dad kept walking until he came to an old building, what once had been a supermarket that seemed to be closed now. "I want you to come in here, Lucky. I want you to see this."

Inside, the building was full of beds in rows. People were sitting on the beds, or they were gathered together into little groups, talking. Lucky could tell, without thinking much about it, that most were wearing hand-out clothes.

"Are these the people who got burned out?" Lucky asked.

His dad nodded. "We've found housing for a lot of people. It's going to be a while, though, before some get out of this place."

"Does the insurance company pay for all this?"

"No. My company is working with the owners of the buildings. They're mostly people who live out in the suburbs—towns like Rockbridge. They can collect on their losses. But these people lost all they owned—their clothes, furniture. Everything."

"If they don't have insurance, what can they do?"

"Well, that's just the thing. They stay here for

now. They get help to get back into some kind of housing. Then they try to start over. Most of them work. They just don't make very much at the jobs they have."

"Hello, Mr. Ladd," a woman said.

Dad turned around and said, "Oh, hi, Minnie. How are things going today?"

"Good," the woman said. She was an older woman, short and very skinny. Lucky could tell that she was in charge, though. "We got in a truckload of food this morning," Minnie said. "People have really come through for us."

"Great," Dad said, and he patted her on the shoulder. "People always do. That's one thing I've seen every place we go. When it comes right down to it and help is really needed, people don't turn their backs."

This was a speech, and Lucky knew it. And he knew who was supposed to hear it. The cynic.

"We do have some troubles though," Minnie said. "We have only the two toilets, and one of them is all stopped up this morning. I have one of them snake things, and I tried to use it, but I can't get nothing flowing."

"Let me have a look," Dad said. He started to walk toward the back of the building, and Lucky followed. Dad turned and said, "Lucky, why don't you stay and talk to Minnie for a minute? This could be quite a mess."

"Yeah, he talks," Minnie said. "There he's got on a suit and tie, and he's tromping back there into the mess himself."

"He's good at fixing stuff," Lucky said.

"That's right. He fixes what he can," and she nodded, seeming to mean more than Lucky had. She had little white whiskers on her lip and chin, and her cheeks were wadded into wrinkles, but her eyes were blue and steady. "There ain't no better man than that anywheres. I hope you know that."

Lucky thought he knew.

"Did he tell you what he done here?"

"No."

"He got all this worked out—found this place and everything. And it wasn't none of his problem neither. The first shelter—the one the city set up— it was way too crowded. So he got this and brought half the people in here. And you know what he done the first day? I said I wanted to help, and he says to me, 'Can you get food?' and I said I supposed I could. So he wrote me a check for five hundred dollars. It wasn't from his company neither. It had his own name on it. And I says, 'Well, you can't be doing that,' and he says, 'Oh, sure. I'll get paid back.' But he knew it wouldn't happen, and so did I, though he wasn't going to say nothing."

Lucky felt the pride—a sort of tingle—start at his neck and run clear down his back. "He does stuff like that all the time," he said.

"It don't take much to figure that out."

Dad was gone for quite some time, and Minnie introduced Lucky to some of the people. They all said the same thing. "Your dad sure saved the day for us," or, "It ain't been so bad since your father took things over."

The one person in particular Lucky knew he would remember was a tall, white-haired man who sat on his bunk with a little dog on his lap. "I did get this out," he said. He showed Lucky a picture of a woman he said was his wife. She was young, and she was wearing old-fashioned clothes. "She died eighteen years ago," he said. "At least her picture didn't get burned up. Most people lost all their pictures. That's maybe the worst of all."

Dad finally came back, with his shoes all wet, his shirt sleeves rolled up, and his coat over his shoulder. Lucky thought about how Dad never bought a new pair of shoes, and how he'd worn the same two suits forever. It seemed odd to think of now that he knew about the five hundred dollars.

"It's flowing," Dad said, grinning. "The floor

needs some mopping up, though. I couldn't find a mop."

"That's fine. We can take care of all that," Minnie said. "Thanks for the help."

"Lucky, I've got another appointment. Maybe you can stay here with Minnie and help out a little. You could do that mopping for one thing."

"Okay. Sure." Strange as it seemed, even to himself, Lucky really wanted to do it.

So Lucky hung around all the rest of the morning and part of the afternoon. He mopped, helped fix and serve lunch, and chatted with people in the shelter. He found out they weren't quite so beaten down as he thought. They were interesting to talk to—some of them funny—and they were mostly talking about getting going again as soon as they could get a place to live.

That afternoon Lucky and his dad rode back on the "T" together. Lucky asked about the five hundred dollars, and Dad only said, "Lucky, we have so much compared to a lot of people. I'll tell you something else. It's easy to give a little money. But look at Minnie. She's been in there working every day, and she doesn't get a dime for it. People who give of themselves give a lot more than people who give money."

"Five hundred is still a lot."

"Not compared to what Brother Christiansen did. Most of the food is coming from him. He says it's from his company, but a lot of it is right out of his own pocket."

Lucky was glad to know that Brother Christiansen was helping. He kept seeing pictures in his mind of the people in the shelter. And he thought of the Christiansens' house, and all the beautiful furniture. "Dad, how come some people have so much, and some people don't have anything at all?"

"I don't know, Lucky. This world has some big problems. People are starving to death every day on this planet. Those of us who live so well could do a lot more. I know I don't do nearly as much as I should."

"You do more than just about anybody."

"No, Lucky. That's not true. There are lots of people in this world who give their whole lives to bring some comfort to the hungry and the poor."

Lucky nodded. It was an interesting thing to know.

His dad seemed to see that the timing was right. "So give that some thought, my young cynic."

Lucky smiled. "There probably never would have been any cynics if the first ones had ever met you."

Dad laughed one of those knock-the-train-right-off-the-tracks kind of laughs, and everyone in the car looked to see what was happening. Dad didn't care at all. He grabbed Lucky and gave him a hug as dangerous as any of the "fights" Lucky had had with the Bunches. Dad could really squeeze.

When Lucky and his dad got off the train, they still had a pretty good hike back to the RV. Lucky was feeling a whole lot better, and suddenly the bright, cold day seemed good. Hanging out with Dad all week sounded great.

"Dad," Lucky said as he walked along.

"Yeah?"

"Where do you think we might be for Christmas?"

"Who knows? You know how things go with us."

"Yeah. I was wondering if you had heard about anything—like any new disasters."

"Nope. Not yet."

"Well, if you don't, do you think the company might leave us here?"

"I don't know. I sort of doubt it. Christmas is still three weeks off." He took a few of his big strides, then said, "Why? Did you want to get out of here quick so we can get set up somewhere and acquainted before Christmas?"

"Well, no. Not necessarily."

"You don't want to stay here, do you?"

"It wouldn't be too bad. You could give me homework. And then I could go down to the shelter and everything. Christmas would be good down there."

"Yeah, it would, in a way," Dad said. "I'd like to see all those people out of there by then, though. That's our goal: to get them housing by Christmas." Then he gave Lucky's shoulder a bruiser of a squeeze. "Hey, I thought you wanted to get away from those Bunch kids, and Michael."

"Michael's not so bad. And maybe the Bunches will lose interest since I'm not at school anymore."

"Well, I don't know, Lucky. I know we hop you around a lot. I still feel best when you're in school, though. It's a hodge-podge education, but you learn things everywhere we go, and it adds up."

"Yeah, but I probably learn as much when I just—"

Lucky came to a stop. He had noticed something as they walked along, and it had finally come into focus. A car was parked in front of the Christiansens' house, and in it were a woman and two guys. Two big guys. Suddenly he realized they were Dr. Kinski and the Bunches.

Lucky's first thought was that she had brought them to beat him up, just to pay him back, though he knew that couldn't be true. She was getting out of the car, and she was waving.

"Well, I'll be darned," Dad said.

Lucky thought that was the understatement of the year.

Dad went walking up to Dr. Kinski like he was her oldest friend, and he gave her one of his handshakes that he could get arrested for. He seemed to sense that something good was about to happen.

The Bunches were now ballooning from the doors of the car like Pillsbury Dough Boys. They didn't look nearly so happy as Dr. Kinski, but then, their faces didn't really show a lot of emotion.

Dr. Kinski got her hand back from Mr. Ladd and turned to Lucky. "Listen, I need to talk to you," she said. "We all three want to talk to you."

"Come inside," Dad said, motioning toward the RV.

Lucky was afraid the Bunches might tip it over, and he was relieved when Dr. Kinski said, "No, we only want a couple of minutes, and then I need to get home."

She looked down at Lucky and said, "Young man, you forced me to do some serious thinking today. And I decided that in most ways, you were right. I like to clear away problems and avoid confrontations. Sometimes I don't take the time—or even have the time — to get to the bottom of things. But when I start accusing people of lying, I'd better have the facts. What I did to you wasn't fair."

Lucky nodded. That had been clear to him all along. He just hadn't expected Dr. Kinski to change her mind.

"So today I talked to a lot of kids. Getting to the truth was like scraping paint off an old piece of furniture. There were lots of coats of ugly colors before I got down to the real wood."

Dad chuckled at the image.

"I finally found out that everything you told me was true. These boys were really the ones at fault. They even admitted it in front of their parents."

Wait a minute. This was getting a little too close to the "too-good-to-be-true" level.

"They have something to say to you," Dr. Kinski announced proudly.

She pointed and Bunch spoke, "I'm real sorry I tried to beat up on you, and I'm sorry I said you broke my hand because I really ran into the door."

The worst actor who ever lived, in the worst school pageant in the history of the performing arts, never gave a more memorized, less-believable speech than that one.

Lucky actually laughed a little. Still, he took hold of Bunch's offered hoof, and he shook it.

Then Crunch recited his line: "Lucky, I'm sorry I knocked you down five times. I'm a lot bigger than you, and it wasn't fair."

Out came his big hand, and Lucky lost his in all the meat.

"I hope that sets things right—to some degree," Dr. Kinski said. "And I hope you'll come back to our school."

That was the bad news. And Dad said, "Oh sure, he'll be there." The Bunches hunched back into the car, and away they all went.

Lucky said, "Dad, that was a big act. They didn't mean one word of that."

Dad busted off a good laugh, and a few icicles fell off the Christiansens' house. "Well, I don't know. It's hard to say."

"Dad, come on. She told them what to say, and they said it."

"Sure. But maybe they really meant it. Maybe when it comes right down to it, they don't like to be bad guys all the time. Their size has probably created an image they have to keep up. Maybe they don't like it."

"Are you serious?"

"Sure. It's really hard to say. Deep down, they might be cream puffs."

Lucky shook his head. "Bernard says those guys don't have a deep-down. I think maybe he's right."

Dad laughed again, though not very loudly. "Well, I'll tell you what, Lucky. We have two choices here. We can believe they're as evil as everyone claims they are, and absolutely without hope. Or we can believe they meant what they said—at least a little. I guess I'd rather believe the second choice."

"It might be stupid to believe something like that. It could get you hurt."

"Yup." Dad let out a gust of steam into the cold air. "Yup, it could. It's sure better than being a cynic, though."

Maybe so. Lucky sort of liked thinking so too.

But what if the Bunches came back? They could still be out there waiting. And that might be the real truth.

# CHAPTER 11

Lucky went back to school the next morning. Everything seemed fairly normal. Some kids still insisted that he had beaten up on Bunch, but others said that Bunch had almost murdered Lucky. Mostly no one said much about it, though. It was old news. The big thing today was that some girl had told a guy she didn't want to go with him anymore. Lucky didn't find that terribly important, though he didn't say so.

When lunch came, Bernard showed up. Lucky had even tried to hide out in the back of the lunchroom. Bernard found him anyway. "Lucky, my man," he said, "how're you holding up?" He set his tray down across from Lucky, and then sat down at the table.

"I'm okay," Lucky said.

"You're lucky. You could . . . oh, yeah, right, you are lucky. Get it?"

Lucky got it.

"So what are you going to do if the Bunch boys come after you today?" He broke into one of his squeaky laughs. Then he added quickly, "Yuck. That meat looks like the stuff we feed my cat. You know what I'm talking about—the stuff that plops out of the can in a big, soft hunk of . . . gunk?"

Lucky decided not to eat the meat. He had been leaning in that direction anyway.

"I saw Bunch on the bus this morning. I think he said he was still going to get you."

"You think?"

"Yeah. I heard him say something like that to some guys. He either said he was going to get you or that he wasn't. I couldn't hear well enough to be sure."

"Well, at least that boils it down to two possibilities. It's good you let me know, or I wouldn't have known what to expect."

The sarcasm completely passed Bernard by. He said, "Yeah, well, it could go either way. He may figure he's got to save his reputation, and—you know—hit you over the head with his cast, or something like that. Or he may be worried about getting into trouble." Bernard hesitated and thought it over. "Naaahhhh," he said. "I'm pretty sure he'll come after you."

"Look, Bernard, the whole thing is over. No one is even talking about it anymore. Besides, the Bunches came to my house and apologized yesterday."

Bernard lost it. He went into a fit of little screams for at least a minute before he could get enough control to say, "And you bought that?"

"Not necessarily. But Dr. Kinski made them do it. And she knows the whole story now. So if they try anything, she won't let them get away with it."

"Yeah, right. And from now on, the sun will shine every day, and the flowers will be happy in the sunshine. It's such a pretty little picture."

Lucky sort of shrugged and let it go. He didn't want to hear Bernard's annoying laugh start all over again.

Bernard wasn't finished, however. "Oh, Lucky, Lucky, Lucky. You may get around a lot, but you still have a lot to learn."

Lucky was starting to eat fast. He wanted to get away. Yet he couldn't resist saying, "Bernard, if it hadn't been for you, I never would have had any trouble with the Bunches in the first place. You're the one who always—"

"No, Lucky, that's where you're wrong. I just—"

"Bernard, why do you always interrupt me in the middle of every sentence I—"

"Hey, you just interrupted me."

Lucky gave up. He decided to dump the rest of his lunch and clear out. Maybe Lucky could talk to a Bunch and get somewhere. Maybe. And maybe he could talk to Michael. But he knew for sure to give up on Bernard. The only thing he had to worry about now was that Bernard might be right, and Bunch might still be waiting for him.

At the end of the day, however, Lucky walked right out the front door. True, he was shaking a little, but he hadn't eaten much lunch. Maybe he just needed to get home and have a snack. For that reason, it might be wise to walk fast.

There were no Bunches in sight, though, and Lucky slowed up once he got a couple of blocks down the street. What a relief! Dad was right. Maybe the Bunches really had meant it. Or at least they didn't dare mess with him now. They knew that Dr. Kinski had some power to make their lives miserable.

Either way, "right" was winning out.

So Lucky was feeling good—until he heard Bernard's voice. "Hey, Lucky," he shouted. Lucky didn't wait, though. Bernard charged up the street and caught up with him anyway. "Hey, dude, are you still mad at me?"

Lucky didn't answer.

"I told my mom to pick me up at your place."

"Why?"

"I just thought we could hang out for a while. Have you got any video games?"

"We don't have a TV."

"You don't have television? Oh, wow." He was silent for half a minute—the thought seemed to overwhelm him. Finally he said, "Well, that explains a lot. That's one reason you don't know enough about how things go down in this world, man."

Lucky rolled his eyes.

"No, really, you can pick up a lot of stuff from television. People knock it too much."

All the way home, Bernard gave examples. After he said, "Take, for instance, those old reruns of the Brady Bunch," Lucky didn't listen very closely.

Once inside the RV, Bernard said, "Have you got any Oreos? I like to have a few Oreos and a glass of milk this time of day. It's good for energy. I like the kind with the double white stuff in the middle."

"We don't have any," Lucky said.

"Oh, that's okay. I'll just take whatever you've got."

"How about a carrot?" Lucky said.

Bernard didn't bite, so to speak.

Lucky didn't speak much after that. He did eat a carrot, though.

Bernard did talk. He explained to Lucky that what he ought to do each time he moved into a new school was make contact with "someone in the know," then find out who the guys were whom he ought to stay away from. He also had a theory that Lucky should never do homework. By the time the teacher really started to put pressure on him, he'd be gone from town again anyway. So what difference did it make?

Lucky did try to answer that one. "My dad says I have to learn all I can. Changing schools all the time, I don't get—"

"Okay, here's the thing, Lucky. This is a good example of what I mean about knowing how things work. See, parents are always going to say stuff like that. Think about it. Don't you forget everything you learn anyway? I mean, say you memorize the capitals of the states or something. At the end of the year, you don't remember them anyway. Right?"

"Maybe not all of them. I still—"

"Okay, Lucky, let me put it this way. Do you care what the capital of Kansas is? Or Tennessee or Hawaii or West Virginia—or anywhere else? And do parents know their capitals? See what I'm saying. Teachers just make you learn that stuff to fill up the day so you're not home driving your parents crazy. That's basically all school is. Once you can read and do a little math, what else do you need to know?"

"Bernard, you're nuts!" Lucky said. Yet he hardly knew where to start with the guy. He was just getting ready, when he heard a rumbling sound. A week before he would have thought that a winter thunderstorm was moving in. Now he knew that sound. It was the rumble of a Bunch voice—still a bit distant from the RV.

"Get down!" Bernard yelled, and he hit the floor. He knew the sound too.

Lucky wasn't going to "get down," even though that had been his first impulse. "Hey, this isn't an air raid," he said, and he walked over and peeked out the window.

What he saw near the Christiansens' house was Bunch—the regular Bunch, not Crunch—and he was walking toward Michael, making noises. And Michael was backing up.

"He's after Michael!" Lucky shouted and ran to the door.

"Don't go out there!" Bernard yelled.

"What are you talking about?" Lucky said as he swung the door open. "We've got to help him!"

"No way, Lucky. You'll get yourself killed."

"Bernard! Come on!"

"Hey, why should three die instead of just one?"

Lucky couldn't believe it. "Look at it this way," Lucky said, jumping out the door. "Maybe he'll be a good business contact." The last Lucky saw of Bernard was Bernard trying to squeeze under the table.

Lucky charged toward Bunch, who had backed Michael against one of the garage doors. Bunch was saying, "Go ahead and take the first punch. You're a big seventh grader."

"Bunch, leave him alone," Lucky yelled.

Bunch turned slowly and looked at Lucky, who ran up to him. "He called me . . . names."

"Not really," Michael said faintly.

Lucky ignored all that. "Bunch, you're supposed to leave me alone now. You promised."

Michael was edging sideways, probably looking for a chance to run. "He claims he wanted to play with you. And all I told him was that he should get off our property. Then he started threatening me."

"He said I was a riffraff."

"Well, he shouldn't have said that. But if you

hurt any of us, you'll get in big trouble with Dr. Kinski."

"I wanted to play football."

Lucky wondered.

"Where's your football?" Michael asked sarcastically. He was getting more confidence now that Bunch wasn't in his face.

"Lucky probably has one."

"So you came without a football, but we're supposed to believe that's what you wanted to do? And on a freezing winter day?"

Bunch looked around, as if to test the air. "It's not cold to me."

"Okay, Bunch," Lucky said. "I do have a football. I'll get it, and we'll play some catch. But please don't hurt Michael, okay?"

Bunch took a long look at Lucky. "Never mind. I don't want to play now," he said. And away he strode, taking steps the size of Mr. Ladd's.

Once his shadow had passed off the premises, a strange calm settled in, like a battlefield after the cannons have ceased roaring.

Lucky looked around to see Bernard, who had finally left the RV and who was now hurrying over to Michael. "Wow, that was a close call. Michael, I'm just glad we could help. You remember me, I think. My name is Bernard Pliney." He stuck out his hand.

Michael ignored the hand and looked at Lucky. "Why did he just leave all of a sudden?"

Lucky was thinking about that. Only one thing made sense to him. "I think he really did come to play football."

Bernard laughed. "Lucky, you've got to be kidding."

"No, Bernard, I'm not. I think he came to play football, and Michael hurt his feelings."

Bernard really cracked up. "Lucky, those guys lie about everything. They always have an excuse."

Michael was the one who said, "Actually, I think you're right, Lucky. He really did look like he felt bad." Michael's tone was full of wonder, as though he had a hard time imagining it himself.

"Now wait a minute," Bernard said. "Let me get this straight. You guys are telling me that Bunch wants to be buddies with Lucky—after all the stuff that happened this week? And you're telling me that when Dr. Kinski made him apologize, he really meant it? And he just came over here for a friendly game of football but got his feelings hurt when Michael told him to leave?"

Michael shrugged. "Hey, I didn't say it seemed very likely. Right there at the end, though, he really did look like he felt bad. Why would he just walk away without knocking someone down?"

"Maybe he was afraid we'd call the cops or something?"

"If he was afraid of that, why'd he even come up here?" Lucky asked.

Now all three of them were silent.

Could it actually be possible that Bunch was sort of like a regular person? "I know one thing," Lucky finally said. "You shouldn't have called him riff-raff."

Bernard was quick to add, "Yeah, Michael, I wouldn't say something like that unless I was sure I could get to the house before he could catch me."

"That's not what he means," Michael said. He sounded disgusted with Bernard. "He means I shouldn't call anybody that."

"Hey, listen, Michael," Bernard said, "maybe those of us who are—you know—a little better off, shouldn't lord it over the more unfortunate. But when these people come onto our property and start trying to—"

"Shut up, Bernard," Lucky said.

"Yeah, Bernard," Michael said. "Shut up."

A long silence followed, and probably for the first time in his life, Bernard couldn't think of one thing to say.

# CHAPTER 12

**L**ucky and his dad stayed around another week, and Lucky spent all day Saturday at the shelter. Lucky liked Minnie, and he had a nice time helping out. He was glad to know that every day more and more people were being moved into regular housing.

Just when it appeared that the insurance company might leave Dad in the Boston area for Christmas, he got an urgent phone call about a disaster in the state of Washington. Rain and warm weather had followed some heavy mountain snowstorms. The runoff had sent a lot of rivers over their banks.

So that meant Lucky would be moving before Christmas. He supposed that was okay. He and Michael had actually gotten along pretty well since the run-in with Bunch. And Lucky had the feeling that Michael was trying to change. He was only jerky about half the time. Bernard, however, was some-one Lucky could put his full faith in. He didn't change a bit.

On the morning that the Ladds had to leave, Sister Christiansen gave them a box of sandwiches, fruit, and cookies, and Brother Christiansen went into work a little late. He and Dad chatted longer than they really intended. At last, they got ready to leave. Lucky said good-bye to everyone, and Emily even hugged Lucky, which embarrassed him half to death and thrilled him even more.

Then Michael stepped up to Lucky and quietly said, "Well, have a good trip."

"Thanks," Lucky said. He couldn't think of any-thing else to say.

"Maybe I'll see you some time."

"Yeah, maybe."

It wasn't much. It wasn't really anything. Yet Lucky knew that in a way Michael was trying to apologize. Lucky was glad he didn't use the words. That would have been awkward.

Michael did have one thing he wanted to say, though. He didn't look Lucky in the eye, but he got it out. "I couldn't believe it when you came out to help me when Bunch was after me. Thanks for doing that." Then he added, in half the voice, "I don't really think people are riffraff. I shouldn't have said that."

Lucky just nodded. He didn't know what else to do.

As Lucky and his dad drove out of the big drive-way and waved good-bye, Lucky felt sort of strange. Maybe he had learned some things, though they weren't things he felt very sure about.

Dad didn't say much until he found his way to the freeway. Then he asked, "Well, Lucky, are you going to write to anyone here?"

"Maybe I'll send a card to Michael some time. And I promised Minnie I would write to her."

"That's good. She'll like that."

"I think she feels bad that the shelter will be closing down pretty soon."

"Yeah, she does. Minnie will always find plenty to do, though. Good people are in demand in this world, you know."

Lucky was sure that was true. But he wondered if maybe it was because there weren't many around.

"Dad, there's still something I keep wondering about."

"What's that?"

Lucky was sitting in the front seat, not far from his dad. He squirmed a little and tried to get com-fortable for the long drive ahead. "I think maybe

Bunch really did come over to play football. Bernard says I'm nuts, but I still think he did. The only trouble is, I don't know for sure."

"Well, I think it makes sense. Even Michael thought so."

"I know. But that doesn't mean he did. He might have been lying again."

"He didn't try to beat up on you after that. And he had a week to give it another shot."

"Yeah, I know. Bernard says he was just waiting until Dr. Kinski forgot about the whole thing. Then he was going to get me with a surprise attack. He didn't know I was leaving so soon."

"Did you ever talk to him after that day he came over?"

"Yeah. Once."

"What did he say?"

"Well, it was kind of weird. He saw me before school a couple of days ago and looked at me, but he didn't say anything. So I said, 'Hi.' I was still wondering about everything, so I said, 'Do you and your brother still want to play football some time?' He got this look, like I was crazy or mixed up or something, and he said, 'Not anymore.' "

"Did he say why?"

"Well . . . sort of. I said, 'Why not?' and he said, 'We don't want to get in trouble.' "

"So what do you think he meant by that?"

"That's what I've been trying to figure out. Maybe he meant that they never really wanted to play football. They just wanted to get me away from the RV and beat me up. Then they decided they'd better not do that."

Dad thought that over. He drove maybe half a mile before he said, "I don't think so, Lucky. If that's how he felt, he probably would have said, 'Hey, we never did want to play football with you. We wanted to knock your head off. And we still do. But now we don't dare.' "

"Maybe. What else could he have meant?"

"Okay. Here's what I think. He meant, 'No matter what my brother and I do, we get in trouble. If we played football with you, you might get hurt, and we would get in trouble. So we'd better not.' "

"I don't think Bunch thinks that many thoughts, Dad."

"Sure he does, Son. He's just not quite as articulate as I am." Dad laughed at himself, with one quick jolt.

"Do you really think it was something like that?"

"I'm almost sure of it, Lucky. I think that kid is decent at heart. And I think you brought out the best in him. I think he likes you. He just doesn't know how to say it."

"Come on, Dad. You're laying it on thick now."

"Well, maybe. I don't think any kid likes to think of himself as a big bully, though. And a big kid like that could easily get pushed into a role he doesn't really want."

Lucky was shaking his head. "I don't know, Dad. I think you're making him into what you want him to be instead of what he is."

"Maybe," Dad said. "But it's kind of a nice thought, isn't it?" He looked over and grinned.

"Or a wrong one."

"Well, sure. I'll tell you what, though," Dad said, and he chuckled. "Let's always remember Bunch as the kid who turned out to be a good guy after all. That will teach us not to make up our minds about people too quickly."

"Hey, the guy tried to squash me three times, and then he sent his bigger brother after me. It wasn't like I just jumped to any conclusions. I had some good reasons to make up my mind about him."

Now Dad was laughing about half loud—which was about as loud as most people laugh. "That makes it all the better. A guy who seemed really bad turned out to have a good side to him after all."

"Maybe."

"Well, let's say, 'probably.' "

"Dad, if you go around always thinking stuff like that, some guys are going to take advantage of you."

"That's right. But it's still a better way to live."

"Bernard says it's stupid."

"Well, fine. Let Bernard think that." Dad sounded serious. "But I've found it's something that works. To a large degree, people give you what you expect of them. You kept trying to use reason and communication, and the Bunch boys finally responded to it."

Lucky shook his head. Dad was stretching things out pretty thin now. "Well, maybe."

"And you stood up for what you believed, and you finally won."

"Sort of."

"Hey, you didn't think much of Dr. Kinski there for a while, but she came through in the pinch, didn't she?"

"Yeah. I guess."

"Well, then?"

"I don't know."

"Look, Lucky, not everyone comes around when you treat them right. I'll admit that. Yet I still think most people do. Take Michael. He's thirteen, and rich, and just doesn't quite know how to handle it all. You were the one who found out that he could respond when someone treated him as a friend—instead of 'the rich kid.' "

"He wasn't exactly falling all over me after that."

"Well, like I say, he's struggling. He'll be okay in time. His parents are too good for some of that not to rub off on him."

Now Lucky was the one laughing.

"What's the matter?" his dad asked.

"Oh, nothing. You just always say stuff like that. Now it's time for your little speech about how lucky I was to come here."

"Well, you were."

"Yeah, right. I met Bunch, who looked big and mean but turned out to be a little sweetheart, and now I don't have to be a cynic."

Dad didn't shatter the windshield with his laugh, but Lucky wasn't sure how it held up against the blast. "Well, yeah, that's about right," he said. "Then there was some other stuff. You met Minnie."

"Yeah, that's true. And I saw what you did for those people in the shelter. That was maybe the best thing."

"Well, no. The best thing of all was meeting Bernard."

"Dad, that guy doesn't care about anybody. He's

completely selfish, and he's dishonest. I would never trust that guy."

"See, I told you that you learned something. There are some pretty bad folks out there. You've got to watch out for guys like Bernard."

Lucky and his dad both laughed this time.

"And one other lucky thing," Dad added.

"What now?"

"You didn't find a girlfriend here. You've got so many girls on the string in all these places we go, life was getting a little too complicated for you."

"Lay off, Dad."

"Hey, I'm right."

"How do you know I didn't fall in love with Emily?"

"Did you?"

"No, Dad, I was just kidding."

"Hey, I'm serious. She's cute. And her old man's my old buddy. That would be great. And don't forget about all the money they have. You couldn't go wrong there."

"Dad, would you lay off? I just said that as a joke, and now you're never going to let me forget it."

"That's right, Lucky. I'm glad you understand me. I liked that Tiffany in California, and Bobby in West Yellowstone, but I think Emily might be just the girl for you. I'll remind you about that every chance I get. By the time you get to BYU, you're going to have so many women after you, you'll be a nervous wreck. Then, when you become the quarterback on the football team, all the rest of—"

"That's enough, Dad. Okay?"

"Hey, don't interrupt me right in the middle of a sentence. That's not polite."

"Yeah, well, it's a habit I picked up during our lucky stay in Rockbridge."

And so it went. The Ladds had a long ride ahead—all the way across the country—and lots to talk about, and kid about. It would be a tiring trip, but Dad would make it fun. Lucky liked being with him. No cynic could be nearly such good company.

As the two traveled, however, something strange began to happen to Bunch. The more Dad talked, and the more the two considered the whole situation, the more Lucky started to feel that his dad really was right. The big guy seemed to evolve. Somewhere around Ohio or Indiana, he had become the giant kid no one really understood—a nice guy underneath it all. And by the time they had veered north through Wisconsin and headed out across the Dakotas, Bunch was hovering around the RV, a wonderful memory, breathing nothing but goodness into their lives. In fact, somewhere in Montana, it occurred to Lucky that he had made a big mistake: Why hadn't he invited good ol' Bunch over to the RV for a sleepover? They could have talked everything over and settled all their differences, right from the beginning. After all, he was really just a big huggable teddy bear, once you really got to know him.

And why hadn't Abe Lincoln and Jeff Davis thought of that? A sleepover and a nice long talk — that would have done it. A lot of problems really aren't as complicated as they seem.

## About the Author

When Dean Hughes was a kid, he dreamed that he would be a writer when he grew up. "Well," he says, "I accomplished the first part; I'm a writer. Now if I can just grow up."

The truth is, he doesn't try very hard. He spends his time writing kids' books, reading kids' books, and speaking to kids at schools. He's also a bishop, which keeps him involved with the youth in his ward.

He skis and plays golf, and runs almost every day. He even ran a marathon a few years back, but he vowed never to do it again. So far, he's been able to keep his vow.

He and his wife, Kathy, live in Provo, Utah. They have a married daughter, Amy Russell, and two sons, Tom and Rob. All three are college students.

*Look for more outstanding books from Dean Hughes*

**Lucky's Crash Landing.** Lucky makes new friends in California and learns to skateboard the hard way.

**Lucky Breaks Loose.** In Louisiana, Lucky takes up football as the smallest running back. He also discovers the pains of prejudice and helps his friends overcome it.

**Lucky's Gold Mine.** Lucky's adventures move to Montana where he learns of an abandoned gold mine, but in a snowmobile trek, he discovers much more.

**Under the Same Stars.** A historical novel that tells the story of the Saints in Jackson County, Missouri, through the eyes of young Joseph Williams.

**As Wide As the River.** The Williams family is expulsed from Jackson County by an angry mob. Joseph struggles to find his place in the world and with God.

**Facing the Enemy.** Joseph Williams must learn the difference between good and evil as he and his family become involved in the Church trials at Far West, Haun's Mill, and Liberty Jail.

**Cornbread and Prayer.** Twelve-year-old Ruth Williams is torn between fine eastern cities and the struggling settlement of Nauvoo. Which will she choose?

**Brothers.** Two brothers become lost during an impromptu winter rabbit hunt and learn true brotherly love and the power of faith as they fight for their very survival.

**The Mormon Church, a Basic History.** Explains the facts, conflicts, and personalities involved in the Restoration in an inspiring narrative that youth and adults will enjoy.

*Watch for these books from Cinnamon Tree
and Deseret Book*

**Enchantress of Crumbledown,** by Donald R. Marshall. A delightful, award-winning story of three runaways and their adventures with Cassie in the refuge they call Crumbledown. For ages nine to thirteen.

**The Lord Needed a Prophet,** by Susan Arrington Madsen. An award-winning book with stories especially for young people about the lives of the thirteen presidents of the Church.

**I Spy a Nephite,** by Pat Bagley. A hilarious seek-and-find picture book for all ages. Find Norman the Nephite among busy scenes from the past, present, and future.

**A Lasting Peace,** by Carol Lynn Pearson. Sol McCallister faces a series of crucial decisions that may result in his death but may also help save the lives of others in the Western wilderness.

**The Magic Garden . . . and Other Stories,** by Greg Larson. A collection of entertaining short stories for young readers, many of which have appeared in *The Friend.*

**My Excellent Adventure: Achievement Activities for Young Latter-day Saints,** by Ray Pettit. A learning program of more than two hundred activities that helps children develop a sense of personal worth and confidence and a deeper understanding of gospel principles.

**The Other Side of the Door,** by Joy Hulme. More than anything else, nine-year-old Dora longs to be inside the classroom. But she's been unable to speak until an operation frees her tongue. Set in 1910, and based on actual people and events.